Hooking Up

Hooking Up

Randi Reisfeld

BERKLEY JAM BOOKS, NEW YORK

THE BERKLEY PUBLISHING GROUP
Published by the Penguin Group
Penguin Group (USA) Inc.
375 Hudson Street, New York, New York 10014, USA
Penguin Group (Canada), 90 Eglinton Avenue East, Suite 700, Toronto, Ontario M4P 2Y3, Canada
(a division of Pearson Penguin Canada Inc.)
Penguin Books Ltd., 80 Strand, London WC2R 0RL, England
Penguin Group Ireland, 25 St. Stephen's Green, Dublin 2, Ireland (a division of Penguin Books Ltd.)
Penguin Group (Australia), 250 Camberwell Road, Camberwell, Victoria 3124, Australia
(a division of Pearson Australia Group Pty. Ltd.)
Penguin Books India Pvt. Ltd., 11 Community Centre, Panchsheel Park, New Delhi—110 017, India
Penguin Group (NZ), Cnr. Airborne and Rosedale Roads, Albany, Auckland 1310, New Zealand
(a division of Pearson New Zealand Ltd.)
Penguin Books (South Africa) (Pty.) Ltd., 24 Sturdee Avenue, Rosebank, Johannesburg 2196,
South Africa

Penguin Books Ltd., Registered Offices: 80 Strand, London WC2R 0RL, England

This book is an original publication of The Berkley Publishing Group.

This is a work of fiction. Names, characters, places, and incidents either are the product of the author's imagination or are used fictitiously, and any resemblance to actual persons, living or dead, business establishments, events, or locales is entirely coincidental.

PRINTING HISTORY
Berkley trade paperback edition / October 2005

Library of Congress Cataloging-in-Publication Data

Reisfeld, Randi.
    Hooking up / Randi Reisfeld.
        p. cm.
    Summary: Four friends—each one the teenaged daughter of wealthy celebrity parents—share secrets, heartbreak, and happiness in Las Vegas, Nevada.
    ISBN 0-425-20522-3 (pbk.)
    [1. Interpersonal relations—Fiction. 2. Wealth—Fiction. 3. Secrets—Fiction. 4. High schools—Fiction. 5. Schools—Fiction. 6. Las Vegas (Nev.)—Fiction.] I. Title.

PZ7.R277457Hoo 2005
[Fic]—dc22   2005017898

PRINTED IN THE UNITED STATES OF AMERICA

10 9 8 7 6 5 4 3

Chapter 1

You Are Cordially Not Invited . . .

"It's gettin' hot in here, so take off all your clothes . . ."

The music thumped and pulsed, as curvaceous and buff young bodies crowded the dance floor, rhythmically kickin' it to hip-hopper Nelly's smokin' beat. From her perch atop her boyfriend's lap on the soft leather sofa, Courtney Bryant swayed in time to the music, and smiled to herself. This party had gotten started all right, and was proceeding precisely as planned. It was the first big event of the social season: standards would be set tonight. Statements would be made. Not to mention paybacks.

"May I refresh your drink, Ms. Bryant?" A spiky-haired waiter named Joey was palming a tray of Platinum Level martinis.

Before she could respond, Liam Mackenzie abruptly crossed his legs, nearly sending Courtney sliding off his lap. He gripped her waist to stop her fall, pulled her closer to nuzzle her neck. Then Liam thrust his beer bottle out to the waiter. "You can refresh both our drinks, dude. *Mi chica* will have one of these"—he motioned to the pearlized martinis garnished with a lemon peel twist—"and bring me another el presidente."

Courtney cupped her half-full flute, the stem between her fingers. Joey, a trusted longtime employee of her dad's, was headwaiter at tonight's soiree. "Just bring Liam another beer when you get a moment. I'm good."

Liam cooed into her ear, "You're not gonna stop at one, are you? What fun will that be?"

Courtney playfully ran her fingers through his golden curls. "I'm pacing myself."

To which Liam responded by drawing imaginary lines up and down Courtney's bare back, tickling her. She squirmed. She'd known the effect the backless Lhuiller halter top would have on him.

So why wasn't she loving it?

When another waiter returned with Liam's beer, Courtney clinked her glass with his and shouted out, "I have a toast! Listen up, everyone!"

The several dozen young revelers in the Sky Box Lounge, on the roof level of Delmonico's Resort and Casino, needed few prods to stop what they were doing—dancing, drinking, dabbling in each other, gambling—and accede to Courtney. What choice did they have, if they wanted to be invited back?

This was her crib, they were her guests.

The strikingly gorgeous honey blonde heiress to the Bryant sports franchise fortune was the only daughter of Daniel

"Slider" Bryant, owner of Delmonico's. This particular luxe penthouse lounge, overlooking Las Vegas's famed Strip, was one of three such salons in Courtney's private quarters.

Courtney waited until all eyes were upon her, then signaled for the DJ to cut the music. With a toss of her long silky hair, she raised her glass high and sang out, "Here's to Liam Mackenzie, captain and"—she stopped to plant a chaste kiss on his smooth-shaven cheek—"supreme leader of UNLV's Running Rebels lacrosse team. Butt *will* be kicked this season!"

A chorus of "Yeah, babys!," "You said its!," and "Rebels rock!" greeted her toast, but Courtney cared only about the re- actions of three specific people—her Girls, who'd been on her ass all week about "being nicer to Liam."

Had her munific-imundo gesture registered with them?

"Liam's da man!" roared dark-haired Reign, hovering over her boyfriend, Brad, at the poker table. She hoisted her cham- pagne glass, and sent Courtney an approving wink.

"The jock rocks!" seconded tiny Taryn from the blackjack table, her cone-shaped hair spikes done tonight in shades of red. She slammed her beer bottle down and ordering the dealer to "Hit me, dude."

Courtney cut her eyes toward the marble-topped bar, where Leesa, who could be the most cloying of her coterie about "doing the right thing," was flirting with two of Liam's teammates. Leesa, who would also be the one person at the party who hadn't heard her.

For her benefit, Courtney repeated, "One more time! Let's give it up for Liam Mackenzie, leader of our Running Rebels lacrosse team!"

Leesa whipped around, accompanied by the sound of her jangling bracelets. In Courtney's opinion, of all her Girls, Leesa had by far the best body—tall and curvy, with lush, wavy hair, killer boobs, killer booty, killer smile.

She favored Courtney with a broad grin. "I'll drink to that," she chirped.

Liam belched. Loudly.

Courtney curtailed her cringe reflex, and laughed heartily. How cute was he? was the message she transmitted to the revelers. All the while silently praying, *Please don't hurl*. She tried to remember just how many beers Liam had downed in the last hour or so. But her boyfriend emitted nothing more than an endearingly sloppy smile and charming tilt of his head. "Uh, oops. Thanks, baby."

She signaled to the DJ to crank it back up, but Liam grabbed her arm. "Wait." He addressed the guests: "I have a few words to say!"

Liam's frat buddy, Tom Delacoste, sitting next to them, laughed. "He has a few words to *slur!*"

A lacrosse teammate added, "Say it, don't spray it!"

A hearty round of guffaws greeted the jokes.

"Come on," Liam countered, "I'm not even close to hammered. I just wanna say 'hey' to my babe, for throwing this party tonight in my honor. You're the best." He wrapped his arm around her waist, pulling Courtney in to him. Which she would have tolerated, if he'd stopped there. He didn't.

"So here's to Courtney Bryant," he shouted, "best of breed and all mine! Mine! Mine!"

Okay, now she cringed. "Liam, stop," she whispered, nuzzling his cheek.

"Don't be modest, Court. Lemme show 'em how amazing you are."

"Not necess—"

"Waiter!" Liam snapped his fingers, summoning one of the roving tray-palming butlers. "Tequila shots all around!"

Courtney had two choices. She could play along, regale in the spotlight, or she could cut him off—with a kiss to build a fantasy on. Though the second had ramifications ("Great Sexpectations," was Taryn's term), she opted for it. Courtney was extremely not up for another moment of nauseatingly public worship.

Liam continued, "Everyone's gonna join me in toasting—" He was midsentence, when Courtney expertly cupped his chin, turned his face to hers, and pressed her lips on his. Before he could react, she'd slipped him serious tongue—teasingly darting around, tangoing with his, and *then* gave the kiss even more intensity. The stealth-smooch rendered Liam putty in her hands, especially when hers began to roam along his inner thigh. The technique was quick, efficient, effective. Courtney silently counted to ten, then threw herself even more urgently into the kiss until Liam forgot all about toasting her.

Mission accomplished. She'd given Liam his public alpha male moment. It *was,* for tonight anyway, all about him. And so long as she was in control of it, it was all good.

"Liam, lambie," Courtney purred, sliding off his lap and standing up. "I'm-a go mix and mingle now. Think you'll be okay without me?"

A momentary flash of disappointment crossed his classic, chiseled face, but then he grinned—and she almost melted. His swimming pool blue eyes sparkled, his sweet smile broadened.

Courtney stood over him now, hands on the hips of her low-slung Prada mini. This one really *should* be a keeper.

Liam Mackenzie was Not An Asshole. He was a truly straight-up guy, a princely prep—homegrown, well-heeled, and acceptably older. Liam was a nineteen-year-old sophomore at the University of Nevada at Las Vegas, to her seventeen-year-old senior at Brighurst Academy, a private, pricey high school.

He was hot, too. Had that whole Greek god vibe: chiseled cheekbones, sun-kissed curls, athletic build—buff, broad, and tall, his best feature being an exceptionally cute butt.

If you lined up their stats—hers and his—on a split computer screen, "match" would pop up. Courtney and Liam were both hot, envied, at the top of their games. A rare find for her.

Courtney's deal with guys was practically cliché. She never had trouble attracting them, but the moment they found out who she was, what she was worth, and the power her dad wielded in this town, they hauled tail and disappeared into the sunset. The sunset, in this cliché, being any random cheerleader, sorority babe, or "sodewa"—socialite, designer, whatever.

She wasn't about the soul mate thing—that'd be Leesa's personal cliché—but a guy who wasn't intimidated by her and/or a jerk, gold digger, social climber, or asshole automatically made the short list of candidates.

Liam Mackenzie came closest to anyone she'd met so far. When not borderline wasted, like he was now, or showing off—ditto—he could be really sweet. He text-messaged, sent flowers, added "meaningful" music mixes to her iPod. In their private moments, he was considerate and intuitive enough not to push her. Bonus: her father approved. That was worth a lot, since Courtney was not so much the rebel.

And the problem was?

Dude, Courtney heard herself channel Taryn, there wasn't any.

Liam reached over and closed a large hand over her slender one. "Come back soon, baby. I'm lonely already."

She giggled, then nodded toward Tom and his buddies Ryan and Goss, over by the billiards table. "Go play nicely with the other children. I'll be back soon."

Soon, she thought, turning away, was a relative term.

* * *

"Let's get it started, uh-huh, let's get it started, uh-huh . . ."

The music had kicked in again, Black Eyed Peas this time, beckoning the rhythmically inclined, or *reclined,* to the dance floor or couches. Courtney crossed over the rose-tinted marble floor, surveying the action in the Sky Box Lounge. Of all the social areas here in the three-story Delmonico penthouse, this was actually her least favorite—too opulent, impersonal, gaudy: too Trump for her taste. Not that she'd ever admit that to the Donald's daughter, Ivanka, a frequent guest and quasi-friend.

She'd chosen the Sky Box tonight for its spaciousness. Along with the fully stocked bar, tiered conversation pits, and DJ stage area, there was plenty of room to add tables for poker, blackjack, craps, billiards, even a roulette wheel. All on loan from the main casino at the Delmonico, all so she could transform the Sky Box into a private gaming party.

Taking long, confident strides, Courtney threaded seamlessly between conversations, threw her head back and laughed at appropriate bon mots, whispered compliments in the ears of some of the girls, hip-checked a few lucky guys. All the while, she kept her dazzling turquoise eyes on the prize: how was the party going? Was it successful? What would people be saying about it tomorrow? She went through her mental checklist.

Sounds? The peels of laughter, storytelling, bragging, clinking of ice in glasses. The swish of cards being shuffled, dealt, chips slid in and raked back, dice dancing on the craps table, the click-click of the roulette wheel, squeals of the winners, the groans of the losers. Excellent!

Smells? Cigarette smoke intertwined with cigars and straight-out weed, wafting from the bar area, commingled with the scent of heady perfume, cologne, and that certain eau de sweat that signaled sexual tension. Cool!

Tastes?

She'd kept the menu simple, albeit with special sensitivity to the revolving diets du jour her guests were most likely to be on. She'd added sashimi for the carb-free, lobster and crab meat for the high-protein pack, veggies for the vegans, turkey and salad for the low-fat crowd, raw sprouts for the macros, black caviar on rounds of toast for the food snobs, and mini crab cakes and oysters on the half shell 'cause that's what she liked. And for never-dieting boys? Piles and piles of mini wieners wrapped in flaky crusts. Judging by how quickly all the hors d'oeuvres had been scarfed down, her tasteful menu rocked.

Sights?

Courtney beamed. Her party guests were gold standard, yet

niche. Invitees had been carefully selected and/or rejected, since scoring entrée to one of Courtney Bryant's soirees was an express elevator up the social ladder. If you were here tonight, you were set for the year.

Tonight's crowd was a careful mix of Liam's pals—college preps who were in his fraternity, or well-behaved teammates—and Courtney's gals, or those at whom she'd waved the "magic wand," deeming them acceptable, even advantageous to have around. Translation: trust-fund Tinkerbells and spoiled scions to business or political fortunes who, like her, attended tony Brighurst Academy.

Visitors to Las Vegas might score an invite if they had celeb-cred—but on that count, Courtney exercised extreme caution. Her best friend, Reign, daughter of a movie star power couple, had "competition" issues. So tonight's bash was a celeb-spawn-free zone, locals only. Meaning: she'd had to say "next time" to the likes of Paris Hilton, Chelsea Clinton, and the Bush twins—though she could never remember whether it was Jenna or Barbara with the heartier party rep.

Insights?

For those, and other business, she needed to round up her Girls. Prying them away from their tables, guys, and games, however, wasn't going to be easy. Nor would she get there cleanly.

"Her Courtship!" Shelby Alexis, who mistook haughtiness for humor, suddenly blocked her way, "Heads up. Someone's in the house who does not belong."

Courtney hid her annoyance. "Not possible. It's totally Platform 9¾." She so knew the girl would not get the *Harry Potter* reference.

Shelby was thin. And not, thought Court, in a good way. The girl was all sharp angles and jutting bones, her taut skin burnished in a fake-bake tan. Shelby furrowed an overly plucked brow. "Platform what?"

"Those who are not invited won't even *see* the express elevator to the party, let alone get in. We don't do security breaches," Courtney said, matching her haughty tone.

Shelby shrugged her pointy shoulders. "Check out the UE"— pronounced *yeww-ee,* it was code for Undesirable Ethnic—"by the elevator. Tell me *he* didn't just fall off the olive truck."

"You know, Shelby," Courtney chided, revolted by the olive truck reference, "if you weren't such a bigot, there might be something to actually like about you."

That wasn't true: Courtney had known Shelby since grade school, and had never found anything to like about the daughter of the woman who ran the most visited gossip website in town. Shelby was a walking stereotype, proving that you could, in fact, be "too rich and too thin." So last decade! But Shelby was a "fremeny"—a faux friend and likely enemy—and Courtney was not stupid enough to banish her.

Shelby frowned. "Aren't you the little irritator-tot? Check it out yourself."

Courtney's cell phone vibrated. A text message—Liam already? The words across the tiny screen read, "How's it going up there?"

Her father. Who never checked up on her in midparty.

"Under control, Dad," she typed back. " 'S'matter?"

"Incoming: Joey sent word he needs help at the bar up there, am sending a new kid. Service lift occupied, he's on guest elevator. Wanted to let you know."

With a satisfied smirk, Courtney confirmed to Shelby that whoever had just arrived was not a crasher.

Which failed to impress. "He's the help? What's happened to the Delmonico's standards?"

Shelby was a snob. But she wasn't wrong. The boy in front of the elevator looked woefully out of place. With his shaggy dark hair, olive skin, and high flat cheekbones, he stood there with his hands shoved into his jeans pockets, shifting, taking in the scene. The body language of a newbie should have transmitted awe at the very least; fear at most.

Even from a distance, Courtney knew loathing when she saw it. Inexplicably, she shivered.

At that moment, Joey arrived, shook the boy's hand, and whisked him into the staff room behind the bar.

* * *

"Read 'em and weep," Brad declared, revealing his poker cards—ten of spades, jack of diamonds, queen of spades, king of clubs, and ace of clubs. "As straight as it gets."

There were six princes of poker at the table. One did not weep, but clucked, turning over a deuce, six, seven, jack, and king, all of hearts. A flush. Which beat a straight.

"Damn!" Brad slapped his cards on the table, sending them flying. "I pull an inside straight, and still can't catch a break."

Courtney had slid over unobserved. She whispered to Reign, "Can I borrow you for a sec? Privately."

Reign kissed the top of Brad's head, and playfully mussed his spiked hair.

"Don't do that!" Brad waved her away. "You know I hate that."

"Bradley," Reign cooed, "I was being sympatico, affectionate."

"Be affectionate somewhere else," he groused. "You're not bringing me luck."

"Hey!" Courtney punched his arm lightly but firmly. "Remember fun? You're supposed to be having it. Quit ragging on my Girl."

Brad looked up churlishly. He didn't like being scolded, but he'd behave. No matter that his family owned enough golf courses to put them in the billionaire category, he had none of Courtney's cachet in this town. Which he craved, big time. Being "in" with her, via his association with Reign, was not something to be taken lightly. As Reign turned to follow Courtney, he reached out and pinched her generous behind.

Over Reign's "ouch!," Brad blew her a sloshy kiss and bellowed, "Later, sweet cheeks."

Chapter 2

Is That What You're Wearing?

Blech, thought Leesa, who'd overheard Brad's smarmy parting shot to Reign. That boy is so shallow and cheap! He's as big a jerk on the inside as he is a slick, deep-pocketed, Polo-wearing, poker-playing prep on the outside. It's so obvious! Why Reign put up with him, coddled him, let him treat her that way *in public,* and then defended him was waaay beyond her. But then again, Leesa sighed—for she knew all too well—a lot of things were beyond her.

Like most of the jokes her friends thought hilarious. Like any required reading. Or the tossed-off references to people, places, and events everyone else seemed to know. As Taryn put it, "Our Leesa, always one twist behind the current plot." Another reference she didn't exactly get.

She wasn't stupid. At least that's what her mom always told her ("Just because you're gorgeous doesn't make you an idiot," was her mom's mantra). Leesa had simply missed a lot because she'd never lived in one place very long. Especially when her mom, a former fashion model (accent on *former*), was between husbands or boyfriends—which translated to erratic paychecks—they moved a lot. Not just geographically, but up and down, too. In Leesa's eighteen years, she'd gone from elegant high-rises to low-income apartments, from mansions to trailers. The worst was the year she and her mom were boarders in someone else's home.

The best? That'd be now.

Leesa Rose Tenley lived in one of Las Vegas's newest, shiniest high-rises, a luxury condo-resort that combined hotel living (room service, housekeeping, concierge, state-of-the-art fitness center, spa, gourmet restaurants, rooftop nightclub) with home ownership. It was totally turnkey.

But Leesa still liked Courtney's place better.

It took up the entire top level of the three-story penthouse that capped Delmonico's. Her envy had nothing to do with one-upping or opulence or grandiosity: Leesa wasn't jealous of Courtney's palatial bedroom and parlor, the tricked-out media center, the kick-back Twi-Niter Lounge, or the eye-poppingly ginormous dressing area and bathroom.

Leesa coveted Courtney's quarters because of the memories it held. Not just Courtney's, but Reign's, Taryn's, and, for the last four years, when she'd become an official member of the Girls, her own, too.

Chez Courtney was their default hangout, their treehouse, a girls-only club where over the years, they'd plotted, planned, schemed, and dreamed, where they'd giggled, and watched X-rated movies for the first time, where they'd gorged and purged, grief-counseled one another, sobbed, bitched, kicked, screamed, vented, and experimented with clothes, makeup, boys, booze, cigarettes, ideology, and images. Where they'd inhaled, gorged on whatever they wanted, and exhaled, purged whatever they didn't—boyfriends included.

For Leesa, Taryn, Reign, and Courtney, what went down atop Delmonico's stayed there. Four girls, one unbreakable rule. You never backstabbed, blabbed, or betrayed one another. And if someone else did? Well, no one else would dare! It was about solidarity, and security, and unconditional acceptance. It was about having each other's backs, even in backless tops.

Speaking of which, Leesa appraised Courtney's as she followed her friends up the winding staircase from the Sky Box level, where the party was going on, to Court's Twi-Niter Lounge. The silky rose Lhuillier halter top dipped just below her waist, falling exactly as it should, exposing Courtney's slender, flawless back. Courtney rarely made the wrong fashion choice—then again, with *that* body, how could she? Tall and slender, small boobed and narrow waisted, haute couture was made for the likes of her! Courtney oozed confidence in every stride, every toss of her shining cascade of honey hair. She stared down opponents, wannabes, challenged all comers with those Tiffany-turquoise eyes. Not for nothing was she the most envied princess in Vegas.

Reign, Taryn, and she, too, were envied. Reign for her movie-star connections, Taryn for her musical chops, and she for her shopping clout. And *all*, for their connection to Courtney.

Irony alert: Leesa, who had an all-access pass to exclusive couture, who could afford any item her heart desired, whose playground was a family-owned galleria, believed she looked good in none of it.

Leesa's mom and step-dad, the principals of Blackwell Properties, owned and operated the string of high-end boutiques that lined the hotel's corridors. The smorgasbord of shops was as unique as the hotel itself. The Delmonico Galleria boasted a mix of classic designers and cutting-edge up-and-comers, plus vintage, funkier, craftier one-of-a-kind custom items—they sold clothes, shoes, bags, and jewelry, gifts and home furnishings. As long as everything was outrageously expensive and sparkly, the Del Galleria was the "it" shopping destination for young Vegas, constantly copied but never replicated.

Kind of like the way other people saw her, Leesa mused. A flair for fashion was deep in her DNA; she was an accessory ace, a makeup maven. Leesa Fashionista they called her. The image pleased her. It was the one thing she was truly, instinctively good at.

She worked it, never letting on her deepest fashion shame: she could diet, and she could work out, but she could not fight body structure. Her hips, boobs, and booty were too broad. She was too "licious" for a stick-straight world and the clothes made for it.

What truly blew Leesa's mind were the people who thought she'd had "work" done, had paid some plastic surgeon, to look the way she did! *If one more idiot downstairs asks me if I got a boob job,* she thought to herself, *I'll hurl.* Like she'd ever add inches to an already too curvy bod. Her daily fitness regime was all about reduction—of pounds and muscle mass.

With a self-pitying sigh, Leesa hiked the last step and followed her friends into Courtney's apartment. Leesa automatically made her way to the floor-to-ceiling windows that overlooked Las Vegas Boulevard: the Strip.

A neon wonderland spread out below her, a hyperreal skyline that never failed to fill her with joy. From the pyramid of the Luxor, to the giant lions of the MGM Grand, from the Paris Hotel's Eiffel Tower to New York, New York's Statue of Liberty and outside roller coaster, the erupting volcanos of Treasure Island to the canals and gondolas of the Venetian, the balletic water dances at the Bellagio pool, even the Wynn's waterfalls, everything glittered, the kind of sound and light show that was music to Leesa's soul.

Leesa understood it was all faux, pretend, a replication of nature or centuries-old European architecture. Nothing wrong with that! This was her *real* world, and she appreciated, loved, and embraced it.

"What's our pleasure, girls?" Courtney asked, sliding behind the private bar.

"Getting back downstairs," Reign retorted, dropping tush in an exceptionally soft, swallow-you-up leather chair. "But since you asked, do me a Ketel One and Red Bull."

"Comin' up," Courtney extracted the bottles from the shelves behind her. "T, what're you having?"

The flaming shades of scarlet-haired rock chick Taryn, already perched on the edge of the swivel chair by the desk, flipped on Courtney's laptop. "You gotta check out the new Eminem video—it kills."

Courtney pursed her glossy pink lips. "Fine, you're drinking Red Bull and Ketel, too."

Leesa was not dressed to actually sit down. She'd meant to

spend the evening vertical and flirtical—at the bar, with the boys—there were always so many new faces at the start of the season. And everyone knew that in a tea-length Chanel, you looked slimmest when standing.

Ah well. There were no boys up here. She was totally among Las Sympaticas. She hiked up her dress and backed onto the pumpkin orange Ligne Rosset couch and stretched her long, shapely legs. "I'll just refill my Cristal," she told Courtney, keeping with the low-cal champagne she always drank.

"So," Courtney said as she handed out the refreshments, and settled herself smack in the middle of the floor. "First, we toast."

"To what?" Reign asked warily. "Please not Liam again. I mean, could ya phony that up any more?"

Courtney looked chagrined. "It showed?"

"Like a whitecap on a black ocean," Taryn confirmed.

"Like a pimple on prom night," Reign responded.

"Like a merlot stain on your white satin Vera Wang," Leesa volleyed.

"Not!" Courtney challenged. "I sounded totally sincere, because I was."

"You played to the room," Leesa assured her. "They were all over it; Liam bought it. It totally counts."

"Believe what you want. It's all about you, Courtney." Reign harrumphed.

"Let's toast Eminem," Taryn injected, already slurping her drink, wiping her mouth on the hem of her boho Harkham camisole top. "Dude is brilliant."

"He's kind of cute." Leesa would give her that.

"In a Dumpster chic way," sniffed Reign. "Trash is so played."

"See, that's your problem," Taryn retorted. "Em was never about the look—he's about the chops, he's talented."

"What's his talent? Stealing from everyone else?" Reign rejoined. "If not for plagiarism, he wouldn't have a single song to call his own! Get it?"

"Got it, forgot it," Taryn said, swinging back to the laptop.

Courtney declared, "Later for your regularly scheduled witticisms, trite and tired though they are. I need a reality check—and not just about Liam. You are the only three people in my life who'll tell me the truth."

"Truth is overrated," Reign mumbled.

"About what?" Leesa asked.

"Well, for one, about the party. How's it going? And two . . . I want to talk about school, our senior year. Potentially, our last one together. Which starts on Monday."

"That's what you pulled us away for?" Reign railed. "Ever heard of text-messaging?"

Taryn, to whom high school was attended strictly on a sporadic, need-to-be-there basis, whined, "School's a crock. We'll always be together. End of discussion."

Courtney bristled. "Mock me all you want. It sure felt like the perfect moment to pull you all away from your various self-destructive pursuits. From what I could see, you, Taryn, were getting creamed at blackjack, Leesa was serial flirting with anything in pants, and Reign was taking verbal abuse from her erstwhile boyfriend. Didn't seem like anything y'all couldn't get right back to."

Reign focused on her glass, circled the rim with her forefinger. "Brad was just in a mood. It'll pass."

"So does gas," Taryn quipped, "doesn't mean you have to suck it up."

Courtney sighed. "Why you let him walk all over you is a mystery to all of us. You can do so much better."

"And yet"—Reign waved them away dismissively—"I don't want to. Do better."

Leesa sing-songed, "You looooove him, Reigney and Bradley, except he behaves so badly . . ."

Reign rolled her phenomenal tricolor eyes—a painterly blend of blues, greens, and yellows—the one feature she'd authentically inherited from her glam mom, and her best, in Leesa's opinion.

As if Courtney had tapped into her thoughts, she said, "Leesa, you start. Tell me what you think of the party so far. How're we looking?"

"For the most part, pretty great—" she started.

"Truth." Courtney tilted her head; her aqua eyes felt like light-saber beams aimed at Leesa.

"Okay," Leesa said, "I'll start with Reign."

Who immediately pretzeled her legs beneath her and pushed herself back, deeper into the chair.

"You have a unique body, Reign," Leesa started.

Code for: chub-o-la. "I just think the way you're dressed, letting all your jiggly bits hang out"—she nodded toward Reign's crop top and low-rider Lucky jeans—"isn't your best fashion strategy. If you want to do jeans, go for Meli-Melo—they're looser, butt lifting, and flatter all body types. And those floaty tops everyone's doing are excellent cover-ups. Do it in lace. Anna Sui does an amazing new top. You can be daring, yet deceiving at the same time."

Reign groused, "I like my jiggly bits. Even better, Brad likes my jiggly bits."

Leesa sighed, but bravely continued. "As for Taryn, kudos for the ripped Rock 'n' Republic jeans, they make a statement, and the keyhole front camisole works. But when it comes to camis, there's a fine line between fashionably flirty and low-down slutty."

Taryn lit up. "Did I cross it? Please say yes, please say yes!"

Leesa frowned. "Then there's the issue of your makeup."

"Go for it." Taryn leaned forward, anxious to hear Leesa's put-down.

"You look like Miss Spider had a run-in with Avril. And no one came out the winner."

"Score!" Taryn pumped the air triumphantly. "That's so the look I was going for."

"What about me?" Courtney said, with a glint in her eye. "How'd I do tonight?"

She'd done amazingly, as always. Except for the one tiny detail Leesa would've changed.

"Courtney, for you I have two words: Sling. Backs."

The room erupted in laughter, Reign guffawing so hard that she spilled her drink all over the chair. "You are such a hoot, Leesa!"

Taryn interjected, "She *would* be a hoot if she was being facetious. So unfortunate that she's not."

Courtney, quelling her own giggles, rushed over to Leesa's side. "They're not making fun of you."

Leesa gave her a look.

"Okay, they are." Courtney whispered, "Slingbacks. One word, not two."

Leesa was incensed. "That's what they're laughing at? It's still the same point. You should be wearing slingbacks with that outfit. And," she added in as much of a huff as she could conjure up, "lip gloss. One word, or two, you ought to be using more of it."

Her friends continued discussing the party among themselves, but mostly, Leesa tuned them out. She didn't really mind if they made fun of her: she loved them all the same. She thought it was brave that Courtney brought up their deepest fear: this was their last year as a team, a clique, the Girls.

Next year? Who knew, really?

She guessed Courtney would go to some expensive East Coast university—she had the grades for an Ivy, so her dad wouldn't even have to donate a new nightclub or anything, though Dan Bryant probably would anyway. Courtney's future was set: she'd major in business, get her . . . MBA. That meant she'd be qualified to take over the Delmonico. A sure thing in a town full of sucker bets.

As for Reign? Leesa bit her lip. Reign's grades sucked, except in electives like film and art, where she ruled. Leesa guessed Reign's parents hadn't discussed it, but she had a hunch Reign might get sent away to Europe for college. Whether she wanted to or not.

It pained Leesa to think like that. But the Girls were about truth, and everyone knew, that was Reign's.

As for Taryn . . . ugh. Leesa shook her head just thinking about it. Taryn was a musical genius, a total prodigy, as accomplished on piano and violin as she was on guitar. What to do with Taryn's inborn ability was where the road forked in

Taryn's household. Her parents were all about Juilliard, the classical music college in New York City.

Taryn had a different vision. It was called "The college of life. Joining, or starting, a rock group and hitting the road." Leesa intuited that Taryn saw her last year of high school as her last chance to change her parents' minds.

Leesa's own road was as smoothly mapped out as Courtney's. Since getting a degree in shopping wasn't actually offered anywhere, Leesa would likely attend the Fashion Institute of Technology in New York. Or maybe she'd stay right here, and go to UNLV. Whatever—her folks *were* going to have to donate a wing or something to get her in. Academics? Not a strong suit. Unlike, say that new Armani . . .

Crash! The sound of smashing glass drew her out of her reverie, and the Girls out of their convo. No one was quite sure she'd heard it—until it happened again. More glass shattering, accompanied by screaming and hollering.

The four charged back down the steps into the party.

The commotion was by the bar, and Liam, trashed beyond reason, was at the center of it. "Don't need no frickin' attitude from the likes of you!" He was shouting—at a waiter! Wailing at him, "We gotta teach you how it's done in Las Vegas, boy!"

Courtney was obviously appalled. Liam had never even been part of a fight, and getting into a scuffle with a Delmonico waiter? That did not compute. Trained waiters never engaged with drunken patrons.

Then she realized who Liam aimed at. This one was untrained. He did, however, bear a killer left hook. He managed to connect with Liam's jaw, and sent the collegiate crashing to the floor. He would have kept pounding, except Joey and his team intervened, efficiently pulling them apart, shouting to everyone, "Disperse, it's over," while pulling the new waiter away.

Courtney rushed over, and leaned into Liam, whose eye, bruised and battered, had begun to swell up. Just before Joey managed to pull the waiter away, Courtney looked up—and locked onto a gleaming pair of dark eyes, as black as an oil spill on the ocean on a moonless night. Her cheeks burned. He didn't look away.

Chapter 3

Movie Star Daughter Unleashes Potty Mouth!

"What were you *feeling* when you cursed out that reporter?" Dr. Sullivan looked at her so earnestly, Reign almost felt crappy about putting her on.

Almost. But not crappy enough to stop.

She deadpanned, "You mean when I nailed the pushy mic-shoving bastard in the knee with my stiletto heel? When I told him who I slept with was none of his fucking business? Do you mean, what was I feeling, *then?* At that precise moment?"

The psychiatrist regarded Reign impassively, not buying her sarcasm, waiting for a real answer.

"I was feeling . . . ummm . . . all tingly, that post-0 glow." Reign crossed her arms. Answer delivered.

Dr. Sullivan tilted her head slightly. Her anchorperson hair did not move. "Reign, I'd like to talk about the incident. Your parents are really worried."

Reign sneered, "Oh, my *parents!* You should have *said* this was about them! Well, in that case, I'll totally open up to you. Then you can psychoanalyze me, and I'll be cured!"

Sullivan frowned. "Would you like to start with your father, or your mother this time?"

Reign laughed, thinking of a line from a Dar Williams song about a shrink and her patient: *When I hit a rut, "try the other parent".*

Ah, but *her* parental units. They were special. You could look it up! Check out *People, Entertainment Weekly, Vanity Fair, In Style,* and *Vogue.* But whatever the publication, the wording didn't vary much:

Movie star Lola Marquez, glamorous and still slinky after all these years (it was she who inspired the phrase "40 is the new 30"), and Academy Award winner, Stefan del Castille are one of Hollywood's longest-running power couples, together since their impoverished childhoods in Sinaloa, Mexico. As teenagers, they came to Los Angeles with empty pockets and a dream: to break into acting.

Fast-forward twenty years: now acclaimed veterans of stage and screen, Lola and Stefan are also revered for their long-standing marriage and their three exquisite daughters. They're prime examples (even the tabloids say so) that not all showbiz marriages end in divorce, and yes, you can be movie stars and still raise "normal" kids.

Reign had sorta blown that last bit out of the water.

It'd happened in Los Angeles, the Saturday night after Courtney's party. As she savored the details, Reign tried to hide a subversive smile, which threatened to pop out at any moment.

Reign and her younger sisters, Starshine and Haven, had

been summoned to Los Angeles to take part in a *Vanity Fair* family interview and photo session for the cover. Reign, Star, and Haven had answered the usual puffball questions: "Yes, we're totally normal. We go to school, we have chores around the house, we have friends. Yes, of course our parents help us with our homework. No, we don't have huge allowances . . ." Blah blah crapola, blah.

Choreography for the accompanying photo shoots hardly ever varied. Lola and Stefan, front and center, surrounded by their perfect family. Usually, Reign was assigned the spot next to her dad, her siblings cozied up to Mom. Sometimes, they switched it up so the three girls were front and center, winged by their parents. At one of the more recent shoots, Reign had been asked to stand behind Starshine, as the photo stylist whisper-clucked, "When she loses the baby fat, she'll be glad we didn't put her up front."

Reign refused to let her humiliation show, made unbearable when she heard her father agree, "Yes, she could stand to lose a couple pounds. We'll work on that, *sí*, Lola?" Her mom neither confirmed nor denied.

Typical. As was being summoned to a del Castille opening, preview, awards ceremony, photo session, movie location. It was what she and her sisters had been doing their entire lives. These command performances disrupted their lives—like *that* was ever taken into consideration. Nor did anyone care that between getting styled, including hair and makeup, and doing the interview and photo shoot itself, the weekend was gone.

Did it matter that Reign had other things to do, other priorities? Not so much. This was not a negotiation. No discussion, no choice. Just be there, and be ready.

The only free time Reign would have in L.A. was Saturday night, before the Sunday shoot. She filled it the same way she always did, by partying with all her heart and Jimmy Choo soles! She knew enough Angelenos to call, where to be, what to wear, who to be seen with.

This particular night it was Fenix at the Argyle, a hot club on Sunset. Wearing a tight tank top and a low-riding miniskirt with a hip-hugging snakeskin belt, she'd had the limo driver drop her in front of the club, winked at the bouncer, and sashayed right past the thick braided rope keeping the hoi polloi out.

As her Hollywood grapevine advertised, the crowd consisted of young actors and singers, plus progeny of the Hollywood elite. A not atypical mix of Kelly Osbourne, Misha Barton, Mel Gibson's older boys, Lindsay Lohan, Tobey Maguire, Ashley Olsen, Usher, Alicia Keys, and, of most interest to Reign, muscled, thatch-haired Oliver Brandon.

The interest, she knew from her last trip out here, was mutual.

Tonight, interest *might* ramp up to action. A wave of anticipation crashed over her as she threaded her way past the bar, stopping to air-kiss her Hollywood acquaintances.

She saw him before he saw her. Sitting in one of the coveted back booths with three male friends, he appeared to be in deep conversation.

Like her, Oliver Brandon was famous for having famous parents. Unlike her, his own well of heritage ran deep: he was the grandson of an even more famous, powerful, and wealthy head of a movie studio. He was what the glossy fawning magazines called "a scion, a next-gen star-to-be," not unlike the way they described the sons of Michael Douglas or Harrison Ford.

Oliver, who was twenty-one, had the world at his fingertips. He could break into whatever career he desired—filmmaking, acting, music, modeling—without so much as breaking a sweat. His name alone was valuable Hollywood currency.

It was also, in certain whispered circles, synonymous with boozing, bad boy behavior, and slacking off. The boy had the intelligence and the creativity to do whatever he wanted. Translation: Oliver was bound either for rehab or for glory. The choice was his. He hadn't made it yet.

Reign del Castille hoped that, for tonight anyway, his choice would be her.

She lingered a few tables away from him, chit-chatting with Ashley Olsen and her coterie, stealing a few glances in Oliver's direction. One of Ashley's friends, Violet Somebody-or-other, understood what Reign was trying to do, and pitched right in.

"Reign!" she shouted, sure to be heard at Oliver's table, "I didn't know you were in town! You look *amazing!*"

Reign wanted to throw her arms around Violet. Mission totally accomplished. Oliver jerked his head in her direction. The smile, wily, curious, and unbelievably sexy, was followed by a "c'mere" motion. Reign had caught everything, but pretended not to. She smiled at Violet and Ashley, and said, "Thanks, you look fabulous, too."

She wanted Oliver to slide out of his booth and come get her. It was so much easier, it suddenly hit her, to play coy, to play boys the way her friends did, when you weren't actually into them. When the object of your confection was nothing more than eye candy, a fleeting, pleasurable hookup—not the one your heart leapt at. Not Brad.

An instant later, Oliver materialized by her side. "So, you

are here," he said, leaning in close to her and giving Ashley, Violet, and the other girls at the table a friendly what-up.

"In the flesh," Reign quipped, turning to face him full on.

Oliver was working the bad boy look. His spiky chestnut hair jutted out in all directions, a bed-head mousse job, his shirt half tucked in, half out, buttons mismatched in the way that made you want to line them up correctly. Of course, to do that, Reign calculated, you'd have to unbutton them all first.

"Señorita del Castille," Oliver was now murmuring, "Would you like to join me?"

Later, it wasn't only Oliver's buttons undone; several of Reign's were as well. Oliver had squished into the corner of the booth, and Reign had twisted herself into him, one leg slung over his, so it rested between his, her arm cradling his neck, his around her waist. What they were doing would, in only a few hours' time, be blasted all over the press as (depending on what you read, or watched on TV) "intense canoodling, swapping saliva, pawing each other, and practically 'doing it' right there at the table."

But just before the stealth attack, just before the nightclub-crashing reporter, and his hidden camera-toting ally brutally ruptured the night, what they were *really* doing was getting to know each other.

Their chatting, nibbling, drinking, and laughter had led to affection, and affection to fondling. Their clothes, contrary to eyewitness reports, were mostly still on, but it was the kind of moment Reign liked best: just before the actual hookup. Her hands wandered all over him, and it made her feel desired, in control. She wasn't, at that moment in time, Stefan and Lola's chunky older daughter, she wasn't the big-butted one, the one who'd inherited her father's stocky build instead of her mother's slender curves, long legs, and luminous black hair.

At that moment, Reign was an A-list hottie, making out in a private Hollywood club with a rich, sexy young scion who could snap his fingers and have anyone in the room. The hookup, which would absolutely follow in one of the private rooms upstairs, meant nothing to her. It brought her neither pleasure, pain, nor remorse. It was follow-through, a promise she had to keep, payoff for the thrill of this moment: his fingertips exploring her thighs, her tongue in his mouth, her fingertips scratching at his chest.

This moment was about to be blasted to bits. It happened so quickly, no one saw it coming. Or maybe the skeezoid reporter had paid off the bouncer, the maitre d', whomever he'd had to. His target was most certainly either Reign or Oliver. He'd bolted right by all the other famous faces at the club, like a heat-seeking missile, to the two of them. And score! He'd gotten even more than he'd bargained for. Accompanied by the surprised screams of the people surrounding her booth, the skeevy reporter bent over them, shoved his microphone between their faces, and announced, "This is Jack Ambush, and you're seeing it here live, on TV's only true expose reality show, *Caught in the Act!*

"Reign del Castille, daughter of Lola and Academy Award–winning Stefan, and young Oliver Brandon, son of Douglas Brandon, grandson of Melvin Brandon!"

Reign and Oliver popped apart, gasping.

"Hi, you two! Sorry to bust in on your private moment here, but we've heard rumors that we might find you two here tonight. And it looks like we've got confirming evidence. Right here, exclusively on *Caught in the Act!*"

In a self-satisfied, booming voice, he declared, "Would you care to comment on your relationship?"

Oliver sobered up immediately, and went for his wallet. "Hey, man," he whispered, "be cool. Turn off the camera. Let's see if we can work this out like gentlemen."

Reign had no intention of doing or being anything with the words "gentle" or "cool" in it.

"Wait—I would," Reign spat at him, "I would like to comment."

"Reign, no," Oliver whispered. "Let me deal with him."

But it was too late. She knew she was going to do it. "Here's my comment. Make sure you don't misquote me—"

With that, she uncoiled herself from Oliver and, for the best leverage, drew her legs up to her chest and kicked the jerk hard with her four-inch steely spiked heel. She'd been aiming for his crotch, but caught him in the knee.

"Ow!" He yelped in pain, grabbing his kneecap.

"I'm not finished!" Reign snarled. "You're an asshole. Go fuck yourself. Put that on your *Caught in the Balls* show!"

Yeah. *That* was a good move: he'd done exactly that.

"Movie star daughter attacks and curses out reporter! You heard it here first! You heard it here fastest! You heard it here loudest! You heard it here over and over and again until you thought you'd smash the TV!"

Unsurprisingly, Reign's parents' handlers had canceled the *Vanity Fair* photo session. Her mother, whose newest movie needed all the good publicity it could get, had blown a gasket—

just before she'd jetted off to the London premiere. Her father had made an appointment for her with Dr. Sullivan.

Stefan hadn't cared that she would be missing the first morning of school. He hadn't listened to her when she apologized, tried to explain the circumstances, assured him it wouldn't happen again. He knew, she reminded him, as well as she did, that this would blow over, be forgotten the minute Mary-Kate went back into rehab, Lindsay Lohan had another meltdown, or Paris Hilton's next sex tape came out. It was nothing, a blip.

Stefan insisted. She was going to Dr. Sullivan's, not to school. She needed help. Now.

Reign begged to differ. She needed to be with her true friends now, Courtney, Leesa, and Taryn. The only three people she could count on to be on her side, no matter what. She needed to be in school.

Her cell phone had been ringing throughout the session, but as she dug into her buttery soft Escada bag, she didn't answer it. Noting it was Courtney, for the third time that morning, not Brad, she merely pulled out a cigarette.

Sullivan frowned. The shrinkess, easily in her forties, was smooth-skinned as a Desperate Housewife. Translation: Reign's family money went right up the Botox needle. How very appropriate.

"Reign, please let's try to dig a little deeper. Maybe you were drunk, enraged with the reporter—maybe you're trying to put me on—but obviously, you were angry. What I want to know is, who were you really angry with, and why?"

Reign rolled her eyes, and took another drag. "It was quid

pro quo," she responded. "The reporter ambushed me on camera, and I decided to give him a lesson in the true meaning of sound *bite*. I don't see what the big deal is. I reacted like anyone would in that situation."

But you're not anyone. Sullivan didn't have to say it. You've had media training in how to handle these situations.

Clearly, Sullivan was getting nowhere with that line of questioning, so she switched tactics. "What about your boyfriend, Brad? What does he think of all this?"

Reign clammed up. Sullivan had no business bringing Brad into the picture. When she'd talked to him last night, he'd laughed it off. Her shrink approximated worry, without worry lines. "Don't you think he cares what you do with another boy? You've been together with him for a while now. Isn't he the one you're in love with?"

Reign knew where this line of questioning was headed. Had she been trying to make Brad jealous? Was she secretly happy it'd all become public? Had she maybe even . . . paid off the reporter to crash in on her like that?

Ha! How little shrinks knew, or could deduce, was in direct proportion to how highly they were paid. She and Brad had an understanding. What she did when she was out of town stayed out of town. They never talked about Reign's away-from-Vegas hookups. They were random. They didn't count. Meaningless, a diversion, a way to pass the interminable time, when her parents ripped her away from her life.

She always came back to Brad. She always would. Whether she was in love with him was not something she cared to share with Dr. Ellen Sullivan. Besides, as a famous sex siren once wailed, *what's love got to do with it?*

She told the shrink, "Here's your tip of the day. People don't do the love thing anymore. It's a bore. And a chore."

The shrink folded her arms. Gotcha! Defense motion, thought Reign triumphantly. Surely the doc would release her, let her go to school.

Or not. Sullivan might've been down, but she wasn't done.

"Okay, Reign, let's cut to the chase. What you did was a huge embarrassment to your parents. On some level, I'm sure you meant to. What I want to understand is why."

She chafed. This woman was so off base she wasn't even in the ballpark. "Take a memo, Doc. Not everything is about them. A reporter asked me a nosy question—about my private life—and I told him where he could shove it. It had nothing to do with them."

"I find that hard to swallow," Dr. Sullivan said.

I could give you some lessons, is what Reign would have said. If she were as horrible as her parents were making her out to be.

Sullivan continued, "You didn't plan for this to happen, but when you did get ambushed, you had to know it would become public. On the day before the *Vanity Fair* photo session."

"Your point?"

"*Were* you trying to embarrass them?" Sullivan pressed on.

Reign was itching to get away. She squirmed, checked her watch again. She'd told the shrink the truth. She wasn't even thinking about her parents at that moment.

Not, she mused now, lighting another cigarette, that turnabout wasn't fair play. Like they'd never embarrassed her? Puh-leeze. Her mother had discussed her cup size in the press; her father had told the world that yes, his Reign could stand to lose a few pounds.

Reign was "thisclose" to telling Doctor Sullivan that if she'd wanted to really embarrass her parents, she had an arsenal of ammo. Like a few months ago when they'd gone from sleek to snarling jungle cats, clawing at each other. Some door-slamming, china-shattering drama that she hadn't been interested enough in to get out her Spanish-to-English dictionary, as they argued in their native tongue. But Reign had deduced something about a boy, some incident with some kid that seemed to be the wedge this time.

Whatever. She also could have told the shrink about her father's hush-hush on-set flings; and her mother's keen interest in a new movement called the Cougars—older women, younger men.

And that really, truly, what had burst out of her in the wee hours that weekend, in a darkened corner of a nightclub, had nothing to do with Stefan or Lola.

"Hey, Doc," she asked, "okay if I pee?"

Closing the bathroom door behind her, Reign whipped out her cell phone and text-messaged Courtney, Leesa, and Taryn. "Be there in 20 minutes. Do not do lunch without me. But if you're ordering from Crustacean, get me a large garlic noodles and Dungeness crabs. Right. Large."

Chapter 4

Punk Rock Chick Does It in the Bathroom

BATHROOM FLOODED. ENTER AT YOUR OWN RISK. BEWARE OF UNIDENTIFIED FLOATERS.

That last bit, Taryn allowed with a subversive smirk as she affixed the computer-printed sign on the ladies' room door, was probably overkill. But dude, it was just too much fun not to include.

As if any self-respecting Jimmy Choo–wearing diva at Brighurst Academy would dare come in. Didn't matter how urgently nature called or a nicotine fix was craved. The chicks at this snob school would opt for the bladder burster over the ruination of a new pair of shoes!

Taryn admired her handiwork. She'd done an artful job with the sign, nice touch with the Brighurst font. It looked typically officious, and officially typical. She'd done it on really short notice, too. Only the first day of school, and already the

"Shame-on-Reign"—as this morning's *E! News* had trumpeted—campaign had begun.

Courtney, Leesa, and herself had to spring into action like Charlie's avenging Angels, to remove Reign from this unflattering spotlight. Time was tight, and the need for privacy an absolute requirement: hence, the closing of the ladies' room to the rest of the school.

Waiting for her friends to join her, Taryn hoisted her wiry body up on the window ledge, leaned back, and lit a cigarette. She'd left her Girls in the school's sunny courtyard at an outdoor table where they'd picked at the sushi and sashimi they'd ordered from the Lotus, a Japanese sushi bar, and, because Reign had pleaded, those garlic noodles from Crustacean.

Lotus delivered to the school regularly; Crustacean not so much. Until someone like Courtney Bryant snapped her fingers. Every business in Vegas that wanted to stay in business, snapped to!

As they'd torn the paper wrappers off their chopsticks, Taryn had handed each of her buds another little homemade gift: a T-shirt with the slogan FREE REIGN splashed across the front in silver glitter. She'd made an identical tee for herself, as well, and now pulled it on over her torn, long-sleeved, black fishnet shirt. Bummer that she had to cover up the black push-up bra she wore under the fishnet, but sometimes solidarity won over fashion statements. Reign, when she finally showed up, was all over it. She pulled her tee right over her head, proudly.

Leesa had been naïve enough to think they could discuss Reign's PR problem out in the open. Yeah, right. As Taryn predicted, they were mobbed within five minutes of sitting down.

First day, remember? The swarming of the wannabes, kids eager to connect with Courtney and lock in a senior-year place in the social pecking order. Ms. Bryant, ever the noblesse oblige social princess, was friendly, even to the poseurs and losers. Just a dappled Courtney smile and regal wave, she sent them on their way without their ever realizing they'd been royally dismissed.

Those students who weren't buzzing around their table were buzzing *about* them. The snickering, mobile IMing was bad enough, but the snide remarks were borderline loud enough to hear.

Worse, that slimy stick of bones Shelby Alexis sauntered over to offer her "condolences" to Reign. Insinuating herself between Reign and Courtney, she was all "I can only imagine what it must be like for you, the daughter of such public, and revered, movie stars. Your life is so hard! You so have my sympathy. And if there's anything I can do . . ." What a crock!

Taryn tuned her out. Shelby was the biggest phony going, transparent in more ways than one. If jealousy had an aroma, it'd be "Eau de Shelby": anything that brought Courtney down a peg made her happy. She was thrilled about the fistfight at the party, floating on the negative vibes coming Reign's way. Shelby had taken a bath in her jeal-o-smell. Taryn had to hold her nose.

Leesa did the dispensing with, leaning into the table. "Psst, Shel, sweetie. Those earrings? The same ones you've been wearing since the beginning of the summer? It's time for a chat . . ."

Mortified, Shelby's hand locked over a dangling chandelier earring. "My dad brought these from Athens."

Leesa shook her head sadly and purred, "There's nothing wrong with being sentimental. But, well, first day of school? What are you really saying? It may be your signature piece, but it's time to give it a rest."

Shelby swallowed. Her eyes darted around the courtyard.

Leesa opened her Hermès bag and fished around inside. She came up with a small lavender box. Inside, a pair of intertwined white and yellow gold hoop earrings. "Go to the nurse, rinse them off with astringent, and switch. Probably no one will even remember what you came to school in."

Shelby let out a relieved, and thankful, sigh. "I owe you," she told Leesa, and hurried away.

Taryn gave Leesa a worshipful "I'm not worthy" wave of her arms. Courtney patted Leesa on the back and said, "Good going." Reign grinned gratefully.

A self-satisfied smile spread across Leesa's full lips. "So, now that *she's* gone, what are we going to do about—"

"Reignie! I feel so badly for you—"

Another intruder had materialized. This one? Not so easy to get rid of.

Reign's younger sister, Starshine, a slinky sophomore with long shimmering black hair like their mother's, rushed over, teary-eyed and distressed, to wrap Reign in a show of sisterly solidarity. "You know you can count on me, right? I can deal with Daddy if you want, just say the word."

Taryn thought she'd vomit. She'd never trusted Starshine—and the point of a public show of empathy was . . . ? Star wanted an audience of her own, and out here in the Brighurst courtyard was choice. Taryn guessed Star's disheveled look—

tangled hair, mussed make-up, unbuttoned Calvins—was a stab at sympathy-chic.

"Has anyone seen Brad?" Reign had asked in a low, anxious voice once Starshine finally departed. Courtney and Leesa shook their heads. Taryn hadn't seen him, either, not that she cared to. She was the founding member of the I Hate Bradley Simmons Anti-Fan Club. Normally she ignored Brad's type, but when it affected one of her peeps, attention had to be paid, action taken.

Reign deserved better than "You've Been Had" Brad.

"I called him when the story broke on Shelby's mother's website, and he didn't seem all that freaked," Reign confided, scooping a forkful of noodles into her mouth. "He was just all, 'Yeah, well . . . you gotta expect shit like that when your parents are movie stars.' "

All four at their table knew about Reign and Brad's "agreement." Three of them believed Brad had okayed it because he was an insensitive prig who didn't really care about Reign. Not only was Reign too blind to realize it, but if Brad got caught hooking up with someone else? . . . she'd be destroyed. Which they could not let happen. Keeping up the charade that Brad cared was the current strategy.

"Maybe he's just covering up by pretending it doesn't bother him?" Leesa ventured.

"It's embarrassing for him, but he'd never admit it," Courtney declared.

"Maybe you caught him half-asleep," Taryn speculated. She wasn't as talented a fibber as her friends. "And he hadn't, uh, gotten the full impact of the thing."

"All that's possible," Reign agreed.

This was ridiculous! Even without the table-crashers, there was no way they could focus on getting any serious plan going—not with everyone staring at them, slyly or straight out. "Let's take this underground," Taryn had suggested. "I'll snag our usual spot. Follow in five minutes, once I've privatized it."

"How do you plan to do *that*?" Leesa had asked, her forehead crinkled.

"I have my ways," Taryn assured her with a cocky, knowing grin.

And now, as promised, she'd secured the first-floor Brighurst Academy ladies' room. The loo was theirs alone.

Ah, Reign, Taryn mused, slipping from the windowsill onto the sink, running her fingers through the scarlet faux-hawk she'd styled and gelled as soon as she'd left the house this morning. She so did not envy her friend. Popular by proxy was how Taryn thought of Reign, sucked up to because of who she was related to, not who she was.

The exact opposite of how Taryn played it: few knew who her famous father was. The fewer, the better. Sometimes, dude, she wished *she* didn't know.

Reign del Castille was envied, and once envied, forever reviled. People rejoiced in seeing her embarrassed, humiliated. The entire school was having a kick-ass day, gossiping about her. Reign could pretend all she wanted that it didn't hurt. But unlike her famous parents, she wasn't that good of an actress.

The bathroom door opened a crack. "It's okay," Courtney reported cautiously from the other side of the door.

"So it's not flooded?" Leesa gazed around warily, sniffing for foul overflow.

"What are you, *new*?" Taryn leapt lightly from the sink and went to meet them. "Get in here," she urged them impatiently, yanking Courtney in first. Leesa and Reign followed.

Leesa wrinkled her nose. "Did you have to be so gross about it?"

"Shit, yeah!" Taryn's lip lifted into a satisfied grin. "Always." Her grin faded as she eyed her pals disapprovingly. "Why aren't you wearing your T-shirts?"

"You didn't seriously expect me to put that on, did you?" Leesa replied, checking her eye makeup in the mirror. "How would it look? My parents run the Delmonico Galleria, and I'm going to walk around in a wrinkled, ripped T-shirt? What kind of statement would that make? Besides . . ." She paused, as if deciding how to express herself, then squared her shoulders and went for it. "Reign, why did you even hook up with that guy in L.A. in the first place? It's so . . ."

Reign folded her arms defensively, "So *what*? So slutty? So below your standards?"

Leesa flushed. "I didn't mean that. I just meant—"

"Save it." Reign went for a cigarette. "We all know what you meant. You don't approve of me."

Courtney, whose eyes were glued to her BlackBerry, interjected, "Let's don't go there, okay? We're a team—"

Leesa interrupted, "I don't like seeing you get hurt, and these random hookups can only lead to disaster."

Reign folded her arms. "Says you—who's never had one! Besides, this is hardly the first time I've played around outside of Vegas, and nothing 'disastrous' happened before."

Taryn growled, "The only thing she did wrong was get caught. And that's what we're here for. We defend her honor, we stand united, we blast balls-out, on the offense. We wear our T-shirts."

"Don't growl," Leesa chided. "It's bad karma. Anyway," she said, changing the subject, "how do you expect *me* to fit into one of *your* T-shirts? It's way too tight and shows every bulge."

"Oh, please," Reign said with a scornful laugh. "All your 'bulges' are where they're supposed to be."

Taryn nodded in agreement. Leesa had the body of a starlet. Okay, maybe she resembled those old-school movie stars, the ones in cheesy spy movies, or video games, where women were voluptuous, curvy, or 'zaftig,' a word her father used. Her parents had a photograph of Marilyn Monroe on the mantel. They'd told Taryn that hers was the ideal body shape in those days. But even today, look at Beyonce, or J. Lo, even Angelina Jolie in *Tomb Raider*. Leesa fighting her own genes was just stupid, in Taryn's opinion.

Leesa turned and, looking over her shoulder, examined her curvaceous butt with a critical and disapproving eye. "Junk in the trunk, much?"

Courtney turned off her BlackBerry. "OK, focus, people. Kudos for the T-shirts, Taryn, they're an artful display of loyalty—misguided though it was."

"Misguided?"

"It'll just bring more attention to Reign's situation, which will be as over as chandelier earrings—as soon as the next scandal bumps it off the public radar."

"That's what I tried to tell my dad," Reign said, "but he wasn't buying it."

Courtney gave a dismissive wave. "People in this town have gnat-sized memories."

"So you're saying we wait it out?" Taryn asked incredulously.

Reign fretted, "But who knows when the next scandal will come? It could be, like, days. Days when I'm sentenced to the shrink. Or worse, the despicable media advisors."

"Well . . ." Courtney considered pensively. "If it doesn't happen soon enough, we'll get proactive. Help it along. Let me go back to my emails to see if something useful pops up."

Taryn leaned against the tiled wall, confident in Courtney. No one knew better how to spin a situation to advantage like the Court did. In her sweet, polished way, she was a mastermind of manipulation.

She dug a half-smoked blunt from her pocket. "Anybody?" she offered, holding out the pot.

"None for me," Leesa declined as she thumbed through the new five-pound edition of *W* she'd pulled from her Hermès bag. "No need for the munchies now."

Courtney looked up from her messages with a disapproving frown. "That stuff will stink up the place and we'll all reek of it."

"That's all I'd need," Reign added with dark laughter, "to get busted on the first day of school after my weekend of behaving badly. Imagine what psychobabble Dr. S would cough up about *that!*" She puffed up her cheeks to mimic Dr. Sullivan's Botox-bloated face and, with a stiff lower jaw, did a pretty good imitation of the shrink.

Taryn laughed and lit a cigarette, passing one to Reign, who was always eager for a filtered joint. As they inhaled deeply, she wondered what Dr. S would make of *her* subconscious if she ever got her psyche-probing fingers wrapped around it.

Parents. Yeah. Can't live with 'em. Can't set 'em on fire.

Taryn's mom, Mynda Lauvin, had been a young socialite heiress who married an aging but world-renowned classical music conductor—Taryn's dad, Ivan Krakowski. Taryn was their only child, and her dad dreamed that she would follow in his grand scale operatic footsteps. He had her studying piano and violin at the age of four.

Reasons to be resentful much? Between her mom pushing her to be the perfect little socialite clone and her dad expecting a violin prodigy, there'd been no time to think about what she wanted. As a kid, she'd followed the program, taking music lessons up the wazoo and dressing in pink princess ensembles. Piano Recital Barbie.

Then she'd met Courtney, and Reign, and began to think for herself. Taryn thought rock guitar was way cooler than classical guitar, violin, or piano. She'd traded everything pink for balls-out punk.

That'd not been a pretty moment at home. Violent battles over what she wore, her makeup, refusal to practice, quitting violin and piano. That's when Courtney had intervened, suggesting that Taryn "negotiate" her parents. She taught her how to be obedient to their faces and be herself behind their backs.

"Why fight when you can manipulate?" Courtney had counseled. "Leave for school early in parentally approved outfits, and come to Delmonico's. I'll have a stylist meet you and get you rockin'—clothes, hair, makeup. What Mom and Dad don't know . . ."

Taryn owed Courtney big time for that advice. Ever since she'd followed it, the home front had been much calmer. And she could emulate her role models: Courtney Love, Shirley Manson, Ana Matronic, Betty Blue, Eminem, Corrosion of Conformity, hometown heroes, the Killers, and the up-'n'-comers with street cred like Mindless Self Indulgence and I Can Make a Mess Like Nobody's Business. She wasn't off-the-hook indie. She totally worshipped the classics, too: Beatles, Bruce, Stones, and (secretly) Sinatra.

These days, she was all about the Bones, as famous in the hard-core punk rock/hip-hop world as her dad was in classical music. Taryn especially idolized their lead screamer, Monroe "Fury" Paige. That dude had it goin' on. There was so much she wanted to ask him, so much she wouldn't have minded doing with him, for him and to him, either. But only if it led to an audition. She wanted Fury to hear her original music. Taryn didn't dream of being a groupie for the Bones. She dreamed of being one of the Bones.

Leesa checked her Rolex. "Lunch ended two minutes ago," she reported, flipping her magazine shut. "We should go."

"Did you come up with anything?" Reign asked Courtney as she stubbed her cigarette out in the sink and fanned the smoke away from her head.

Courtney shook her head. "No. We're in a dearth-of-gossip moment. If nothing juicy happens by end of day, we have to create something. Nothing buries a scandal like a new one."

"You mean, make something up, a rumor about some-one—even if it's, uh, false?" Leesa asked, doubtfully.

"I'm not sure what we need yet," Courtney conceded. "Could be something really simple. Like, it's possible people don't really know about Shelby's ana issues, or . . . mmm . . . Brad's gambling problem."

Reign scowled. "He does not have a gambling problem!"

Leesa frowned. "Why assume Shelby's got an eating disorder? Maybe she's just narrow-boned."

"And maybe, Leesa"—Taryn couldn't help herself—"when your IQ reaches fifty, you should sell."

Reign howled, Courtney glared—and Leesa knotted her brow in confusion.

"Of course," Courtney mused, "we could go with the always-reliable someone pretending to be who he or she isn't—you know, someone feigning wealth when in fact the family's in deep debt, or jail bound. We could do illicit affairs, shtupping of the hotel staff . . . spread the rumor that the basketball team's on steroids—though that's hardly news—or someone at school had a baby over the summer. It shouldn't be hard. We've gotta make people stop gossiping about Reign."

Leesa'd had enough. "See you guys." She pulled open the door.

"Wait up," Courtney called, dropping her BlackBerry into her bag. Reign followed her to the door, then turned to wait for Taryn.

"You go ahead," Taryn told her. "I want to fix my eyeliner."

"It looks fine," Reign told her.

"Wiping it off is the only fix you need," was Leesa's parting shot.

"Yeah, well, I want to make it thicker, blacker," she insisted.

Once she was alone, Taryn took the blunt out again and lit

up. She'd made it through her morning classes, a feat in itself. Other than her Girls, she had nothing to say to these brainless Brighurst brats, female or male. The guys were afraid of her; they wouldn't touch her with a ten-foot pole and she wouldn't want them to. She snickered, coughing out a cloud of smoke. As if one of them *had* a ten-foot pole.

And her classes! Could they be more meaningless?

Life was what she craved—real life. Not this obscene parade of soulless overprivileged shitheads.

As the pot kicked in, her senses heightened. The border of black tile wrapping around the room glowed with a deep sheen. She'd never noticed before how the green flecks within it gave the tile a fathomless quality, like she was looking into the far reaches of space.

She moved to the mirror and gazed at herself. She wished she wasn't so small boned, such an urchin. It would be nice to be tall and striking like Courtney, but she didn't hate the way she looked. She pulled the Free Reign T-shirt off to once again reveal the black bra below the fishnet shirt. Even though she was compact, she had a kickin' bod. Might as well show it off.

Taryn leaned over the sink and studied her face. It was all right, really, fine boned with big eyes—the faux-hawk made them look even bigger. Someone had once compared her to the Japanese anime characters in graphic novels and cartoons like Yu-Gi-Oh!, all spiked hair and huge eyes. But they definitely needed more liner, no matter what Leesa Fashionista dictated.

Fishing a black liner from her canvas khaki studded bag, she began rimming her eyes as steadily as she could manage.

She knew the blunt made her hand unsteady, but it felt more precise than ever before. And dude, she actually looked sexier than before.

"You look hot, T," she told the girl in the mirror. "I should always get stoned before putting on my makeup," she decided out loud and something about this idea suddenly struck her as hysterically funny. She began laughing so hard she had to clutch the lip of the sink to keep from falling over.

Taryn felt too sexy to waste another minute at Brighurst. "Seize the day!" she advised her mirror image. Weaving slightly, she pulled down the homemade Do Not Enter sign and tossed it on the floor as she left the ladies' room.

Taryn was expert at sneaking out of school; she'd done it countless times. She made a pit stop at her locker, to retrieve her Yamaha electric six-string, slung the ax over her shoulder, and was just about to head for the emergency exit when she felt a pair of eyes on her. She whirled. Some random dude, dark and lanky, was just shutting his locker. Their eye contact was too fleeting for Taryn to process. She needed every compromised brain cell she could summon to remember how to disable the emergency exit switch, and bolt out.

* * *

"Bangers on Eleventh Street," she told the cab driver.

Bangers was a narrow little bar where kick-ass musicians got it together with local rockers.

Courtney hated the place. The hotel heiress knew every joint in the city, good, bad, or mad-ugly. Her friend decreed it, "A total slummy dive."

That was all Taryn had needed to hear.

Bangers had become her secret hangout, a place she could go to play her guitar in the hopes of meeting the kinds of musicians who'd appreciate it. The ticking of the taxi meter reminded her that her clock was ticking too. If she didn't get anything going by June, she'd be headed to Juilliard in September.

The driver seemed psyched with his tip as she stepped rockily out onto the street and down the stairs into the dark, cave-like club. The noxious odor of spilled beer emanated from the floorboards and mixed with the Freon of the air conditioner. The walls were lined with autographed photos of faded bad boy celebs—Mick Jagger, Keith Richards, Vince Neil, Tommy Lee, Gene Simmons. And a couple of bad girls as well—Chrissie Hynde, Shirley Manson, Courtney Love.

Weirdly, Taryn suddenly felt very alone.

A couple of rough-looking guys were at one table, but other wise? The place was empty.

It hit her: Hello, it's, like, 1 P.M. Ridiculously early for any real musicians to be here, unless they were still partying from the night before. The bartender, a reedy dude in a white beater tee and jeans came out from the back, took one look at her, and put his hands on his hips.

Taryn waved, relieved to see someone she knew. "Hey, Lou, howzit hangin'?"

"Shouldn't you be in school, little girl?" Lou said.

"Get all the school I need right here at Bangers," she replied.

He shook his head, grabbed a cloth, and began wiping down the bar.

Taryn motioned toward the minuscule stage area. "Okay if I hang out, set up and go over some riffs?"

"S'all yours—knock yourself out."

"And," Taryn added over her shoulder, as she bent to plug in her guitar, "how 'bout a little liquid refreshment? Helps loosen up the music muscles."

The bartender frowned. "You're underage."

"And you're underpaid," Taryn fired back, whipping four crisp $50 bills out of her pocket. "I won't tell if you don't."

She downed the shot in one long, hot swallow. The jolt of tequila ran up her sinus cavity and blasted her out of her reefer haze. At least the first one did. The second two jazzed her into an edgy, restless state. She wished someone else would arrive, tried to remember which bands were in town this week.

She hadn't planned what to play, but soon the fist-pumping thrum of her guitar filled the room. It was rough, and raw, and restless, and it was one of her own songs. It was everything Taryn felt on the inside. "Assassin Heart." That was a good name for it.

Taryn's head had been bent, her ear pressed to the guitar. So she really had no idea how long the tattooed stranger had been watching.

The scruffy beginnings of a beard, long, stringy hair, many tattoos with an especially striking thorny swirl at his jugular. Blue eyes peered out of a tanned face and exuded appreciation for her form. Twenty . . . twenty-five at the most.

"A rock chick who can play and do shots at the same time," he said. "I've died and gone to heaven."

Ewww. Her stomach turned. This was so not what she'd been hoping for. This guy is—

"I'm Dirk," he told her, holding out a meat slab of a hand. "I'm with the Bravery; we're playing Mandalay Bay tomorrow."

"You're with the band?" Taryn narrowed her eyes. She knew every member of the Bravery—who didn't?—she couldn't recall any Dirk.

"I do backup licks," he informed her, letting his tongue roam around his lip. "All kinds." As if she didn't get the message.

Taryn's stomach twisted. Dirk was a dirtbag. But that didn't mean she wouldn't flirt with him. Especially if he was an all-access pass to the Bravery.

She kicked up a corner of her lip in a way that she hoped was sexy and knowing. "Been on the road with them long?"

"Since the beginning of the tour." He eyed her carefully. "Makes a guy thirsty. And lonely for the company of a cute chick like you. You ain't half bad on guitar either."

In response, Taryn played the first verse of "An Honest Mistake," one of the Bravery's big hits.

He tilted his head, impressed, then ordered two more shots from the bar. "I'm buyin'," he said to her, "if you're drinking and playing."

She remembered drinking the next two shots and throwing back the rest of her Red Bull. She remembered that on her way to the bathroom, Lou, the bartender, whispered something in her ear. Sounded like, "He's trouble. Bad idea to get friendly." To which she recalled responding, "Ah, Lou-E, Lou-I, I can handle it."

She remembered quizzing Dirk about the band and their music, leading up to the part where she'd ask about her own music, did he think it was good, did he think the Bravery would give her an audition?

Dirk deflected her questions. He seemed to have other things on his mind. After a while, he kinda began to look better. Those blue eyes were piercing, the tan attractive. If she hooked up with him, she reasoned, it'd be at the hotel. Where the rest of the band was. Could she go through with that? Despite her frontin', it would be a first.

Then, Dirk not-so-gently took hold of her guitar, pulled it away from her body, the guitar strap over her head. " 'Nuff with the string-along," he said gruffly. "Let's play for real now."

For a split second, Taryn actually thought he was going to take out his own guitar, or use hers to play some riffs. But that wasn't what he wanted to show her. Those blue eyes, a moment ago piercing, now bore right into her chest. The push-up fishnet was doing its thing.

She wanted to be cool. She would be cool. But even through the tequila and the weed, her heart hammered. She could not stomach him a moment longer, even if it did mean a trip back to the hotel, an audience with the band.

Abruptly, Dirk stood and pulled her up with him. He grabbed her wrists and started toward the back, where the restrooms were. "Let's go somewhere private," he urged. "A quick BJ, that's what I'm feeling."

Maybe it was the tequila. It might have been the drunken disdain in his voice, or maybe it was her shock and hurt at his outright disgusting suggestion. For whatever reason, it just happened: spontaneous projectile spewing. The contents of her last Red Bull and tequila splashed all over his face.

Like an angry bull he charged her. Without thinking, Taryn grabbed the neck of her guitar, and went to whack him over the head. Only she was too short, too drunk, and too stoned. Whipping the ax around, the only thing she managed to hit was herself, right in the face.

The dirtbag howled with laughter. "Go back to kindergarten, ya little poseur. Only big girls play with the big boys. And, by the way, I lied: I ain't with the Bravery and your music sucks."

Chapter 5

Hotel Heiresses' Daydreams . . . Are Wet

In her spankin' new DKNY bikini, Courtney luxuriated in the dry heat of late afternoon sun, stretching out on the full-length lounger beside the Lazy River, one of the Delmonico's six waterfront areas. She and her Girls could have gone to the big pool, which featured in-water gambling and a blended drinks bar, or the wave pool with its water slides, the man-made beach, or the cozy Jacuzzi built into faux boulders and surrounded by waterfalls, but the Girls normally opted for this one, the least crowded because it was tucked away in a far corner of the resort. Of course there were the requisite cabanas and cabana boys, plus eye-candy waiters armed with slushy drinks, a bar that stocked only top-shelf liquor, wine, and champagne, and the hottest lifeguard on duty.

Not that Courtney cared much for looking at anything or anyone at the moment.

In fact, from behind her Gucci sunglasses, her eyes were shut. All the better to block out everything, even Reign, Leesa, and Taryn, who were sunning alongside her. She craved the black screen of her closed eyes, a blank canvas on which to replay a memory that she'd been obsessed with since the day it happened. Same as the Reign day, in fact.

Okay, so she'd lingered too long on her cell phone. But Liam couldn't stop apologizing for that bizarre fist-flinging fight at her party on Friday. "I blame myself, Courtney. It was so stupid! Get into it with a lowly waiter, of all people? I was drunk, and I'm just so, so sorry. It'll never happen again."

Liam had sent flowers to her suite on Saturday. He totally owned his bad, and Courtney forgave him. He seemed to need lots of reassurances of said forgiveness. No way could she blow him off, or show her annoyance with his "lowly waiter" remark.

Better people than him, her dad always said, work as waiters, and staff the hotels and casinos. Dan Bryant valued people for who they were, not for how much money they had, or their current station in life. He'd instilled those values in his only daughter.

The bell had rung, and if she was going to get to class before being called out tardy, she had to haul tush. She was checking her Coach watch when some random guy did a drive-by—he bumped into her, knocked her Psych text out of her arms, and kept going.

"Hey!" she cried irately at the retreating male figure. "Way to be rude!"

The offender turned, looking as though she'd just awakened him from a preoccupation so deep that he was barely aware of his surroundings. "Oh, shit, did I do that?" he murmured, coming back toward her.

Their eyes locked. Her cheeks burned. And her heart pounded. If not for her excellently applied makeup, she might have rubbed her eyes. Vegas was known to cause mirages. But this was no hazy vision out on the horizon.

This was real. This was near. This was here, in her school corridor. This was . . . him?!

The waiter. *That* waiter from the party, the one who'd gone at it with Liam, the one with whom she'd had a briefest of stare-affairs.

What was he doing at Brighurst? A battered book bag slung over one shoulder made him resemble . . . a student?

She studied him as he scooped her Psych text off the floor, struck once again by his shaggy dark hair, olive skin, high flat cheekbones.

Shouldn't she be the loyal girlfriend and say something cutting to him, a scathing reprimand for whaling on Liam, maybe threaten to have him fired? But it was all Courtney could do to control her shaking.

Saying nothing, she took the book from him. Only . . . their hands touched during the transfer. His skin was rough. It took her aback. Only . . . not in a bad way. The touch seemed to affect him, too, because he looked at her—stared, really! There was recognition in his dark eyes and something else. Appreciation? No, it was something else. More . . . primal. Courtney couldn't believe she'd even thought that! She wanted to turn on her heel, regally, and dash off to class. But she couldn't.

His lips parted in the faintest smile, revealing a line of dazzling white teeth. His demeanor was almost predatory! She was dimly aware that they were standing too close together, closer than two strangers should, but she didn't care. For a moment, she pictured him pulling her into a steamy clutch. She wouldn't have stopped him. The thought both horrified and excited her.

And then he was gone, heading off down the hall. It left her nearly panting with frustration, as though he'd brought her to the brink of something, and then abruptly, inexplicably abandoned her.

Abandoned *her*—Courtney Bryant! No one walked away from her. She realized she was trembling and she didn't know if it was with fury or from disappointment.

The scene rewound again and again in her head. Try as she might to banish it, to tell herself it had been nothing—just a stupid collision in the hallway—it kept playing like a loop.

"Courtney!"

Someone was yelling her name. She had just hit "replay" and it was irritating to be pulled out of her reverie so abruptly. But Taryn's tone was insistent.

Courtney rolled on her side, lifting onto one elbow. "What?" she asked with an edge in her voice.

Taryn lounged beside her in a black, silver-studded D&G bikini and gigantic aviator-style shades. Her short red hair was disheveled, spiking in every direction. "Finally! Thank you," she said, obviously irritated too. "I don't know where you were, but it's the third time I tried to get your attention."

"Sorry. What's up?" Courtney asked her.

"Are you sure Fury is really coming to Delmonico's?"

"Yes!" Courtney cried, completely exasperated. She had answered that same question at least ten times since this afternoon when she'd first told Taryn that the Bones had signed to perform at Delmonico's. They'd been just about to ink a deal at the Hard Rock when her dad, after conferring with her, had made them a better offer.

Courtney knew it was an awesome coup, but to Taryn it was completely off the hook. Too good to be true. "Are you totally sure? I mean, you talked to their manager yourself, right?" Taryn kept on.

"Yes! Yes! Yes! The Bones are definitely, solidly booked. They'll be here next month," Courtney replied. "But you may not get to see them since you're driving me crazy and if you ask me one more time I'm going to kill you. Then you won't be able to see them because you'll be dead."

"Whoa! Chill! I just can't believe Fury is actually coming here!"

"What *I* can't believe—at all—is that you cut out the first day of classes—right after our bathroom break!" Leesa said, her chest bursting out of her striped, halter-top Nautica bikini; her abs washboard flat and fit, her hips jutting. "And then you missed the second day of school altogether!"

"The real head-scratcher is you in the middle of some random bar fight—" Reign added as she tugged down the bottom of her Ralph Lauren one-piece. "In a downtown skeezehall. What were you even doing there?"

Taryn slid her aviator shades down the bridge of her nose. "Hypocritical much? You do your hookup thing, I do my mash-up thing. At least I didn't get . . . Caught in the Act."

Reign flipped over on the chaise lounge, her back to Taryn. "Point taken."

Courtney winced. Middle of a bar fight? An innocent bystander? There was more to the story, for sure. If Taryn's tightly wound father ever found out he would not just haul her off to the shrink as Stefan del Castille had done, following Reign's public display.

Taryn's parents were old school. They'd drop-kick their only child's butt all the way to some tough-love boot camp. They'd get her the hell out of Brighurst.

Covering for Taryn had vaulted to priority one. It'd bumped the Reign sitch to number two.

Luckily, Leesa had her own way of covering Taryn's ill-gotten souvenir. "Prescriptives," Leesa'd announced. "We're selling this new advanced formula in the Avena-Mulkana boutique. No one will ever know the bruise is there."

A fleeting look of disappointment crossed Taryn's face. To her, the bruise was a medal of honor, a battle scar in her constant bid for musical street cred. So misguided!

But what had really happened? Taryn described it as a minor scuffle. Could be she didn't remember. Last night she'd stumbled into Courtney's place, a complete train wreck. When Courtney had pressed for info, all Taryn had been able to do was cry inconsolably before passing out on a couch in Courtney's bedroom, leaving Court to call Taryn's parents and let them know she was okay, throw a blanket over her, and let her sleep.

The morning had brought a Taryn debilitated by a crashing tequila hangover, complete with a brain-blasting headache. Courtney had tried to rouse her for school, but Taryn only pulled the covers over her head and turned away.

Courtney let her stay there.

At Brighurst, Courtney had kept a sharp eye out for waiter-boy, but didn't see him. That afternoon, Reign and Leesa accompanied her back to Delmonico's, where they found Taryn still lying in bed looking decidedly pale and hung over and staring listlessly at MTV on Courtney's plasma TV.

The girls had been changing into bathing suits to head down to the pool, when Courtney's phone rang. It was her dad, confirming that the deal had been done.

"It's official! The Bones are coming to Delmonico's," she announced, hanging up her bedroom phone.

"The Bones!" Taryn had shouted. "You rule! You'll get me an all-access pass, a backstage pass, everything, right?"

Courtney had smiled. "I'll do what I can, T, you know that."

Now Courtney shook her head woefully as Taryn pushed back her sunglasses, flipped up her headphones, and began rocking to the beat of whatever was streaming through on her iPod. She was pushing harder and harder lately, testing the furthest limits of her edgy persona. So far she had been lucky but Courtney didn't want to think about what might happen when her luck ran out. If that happened, Taryn's parents would be the least of her problems.

Taryn hooking up with Fury of the Bones was a really bad idea: a thought Courtney decided best kept to herself. Until she figured out what to do.

Reign stood and stretched. "Finally," she said as a poolside waiter came over with a tray containing four fluted glasses of Cristal. Swooping one off the tray, she downed most of it in a gulp. "I know Taryn's barroom brawl trumped my little scandal, but Court, any brain flashes about that rumor thing?" she asked.

"Done," Courtney told her with a satisfied smile.

"Really?" Reign asked, eyebrows arched.

"I did it this morning. I called the *Las Vegas Review-Journal* and gave an anonymous tip to the society columnist. I said that someone at Brighurst—maybe a newcomer, maybe not—is hiding a huge secret. He or she has a dubious past, maybe even a dangerous one. I said I was calling in the public interest. I think it's going to appear in the 'On the Scene' column."

"And they just believed you?" Reign questioned.

"The woman I gave the tip to is an assistant. She used to do press releases for Dad before she went to work for the paper. I told her my name but said I wanted to stay anonymous. She trusted the tip because it came from me," Courtney revealed.

"That is crazy brilliant!" Leesa praised her. "Who has the secret?"

Courtney shrugged. "How do I know? No one, maybe."

Taryn drawled, "She. Made. It. Up. That's why they call it a rumor, not 'for real.' We talked about this yesterday, remember?"

"And yet," said Reign, licking the rim of her champagne flute, "it could be true after all. There is a newcomer at Brighurst . . ."

She turned to Courtney, as if to get the OK.

Courtney shrugged.

"The waiter? From the other night at the party? The guy who threw down with Liam? He turns up in my Econ class!" Reign told them. "He's new this year. Name's Jake Martinez."

"Are you kidding?" Leesa cried.

"Oh *yeah*," Taryn declared, "I *thought* I saw someone familiar yesterday, too. I was leaving the school, pretty stoned, so I wasn't too sure."

"So how's he affording it?" Reign wondered out loud. "Is there some kind of federally funded 'No Waiter Left Behind' program we don't know about?"

"Good one!" Taryn laughed, but Courtney didn't find it funny.

"You think he's in some kind of scholarship program?" Leesa asked.

"That's what I want to know," Courtney admitted, being careful not to reveal just how *badly* she wanted to know.

Reign chuckled mischievously. "And when you get the dirt on him, you can make his life miserable—a payback for his slugfest with Liam."

"Something like that," Courtney agreed noncommittally. Let them think what they liked. She would not admit her fledgling obsession with the waiter . . . Jake. It was probably just a passing thing, anyway; a fire that would burn itself out before long. Like a shooting star, a meteorite, a bright blinding flash in the sky. It *had* to be.

The combo of the sun and her second glass of Cristal made Courtney drowsy. Soon she drifted away, like a gently rocking raft in the pool, into a lovely, lovely dream. She was lying on her back, on a staircase at school. Blinding sun streamed in from the tall window nearby. Jake was there, kissing her, his warm mouth moving from her throat down to her shoulder. She sighed in the throws of a full-throttle turn-on.

He began to pull off his white shirt as he knelt over her, revealing a lean, well-muscled physique. She writhed seductively there on the stairs, barely able to wait another second for him to take off his shirt.

And then suddenly the staircase began to shake! She gripped the rails as her waiter fell backwards, tumbling away from her.

"Courtney, wake up!" Taryn's voice cut into the dream. Her friend was shaking her arm insistently. "I'm splitting."

Courtney bolted upright on her lounger, confused to find herself back beside the pool. Returning gradually to reality, she blinked into the strong sun blasting over Taryn's shoulder. "Leesa and Reign had to go and I should get home and at least show my face to pacify the parents," Taryn told her.

"Okay," Courtney agreed, her voice still thick with sleep. "But shouldn't you hit Leesa's store first, get that cover-up stuff? How are you going to explain the bruise on your cheek?"

"Never explain, never complain," Taryn said flippantly as she hoisted her tote onto her shoulder. "I'll put purple shadow around the other eye and no one will notice the difference, make it look like it's supposed to stand out."

"That might work," Courtney conceded.

Taryn's expression turned more serious. "Thanks for . . . you know . . . letting me wash ashore at your place."

Courtney nodded. "No lectures, but . . ."

"I'm a big girl," the elfin Taryn assured her, confident but a little sad. "I can deal."

Courtney raised her eyebrows skeptically. It would take more than a friendly warning to deflect Taryn from the path she was so clearly hell-bent on following.

"Peace out," Taryn said, turning to leave. She took two

steps and then turned back with a wicked grin. "If you're quick, maybe you can get back to that dream you were having. I don't know what was going down but you were digging the hell out of him—whoever he was."

Courtney fought down the warmth of a red blush that threatened to engulf her. "I guess Liam is the man of my *dreams,* after all," she bluffed.

When Taryn was gone, Courtney dove into the pool and ferociously freestyled a few laps to throw off the effects of champagne and her nap. Then she slipped on her Cole sandals and Lacoste cover-up and took the private express elevator to her penthouse.

* * *

When she entered the immense suite her dad used as his office, he was just finishing up a business call. The room had recently been redone, much to Courtney's chagrin, and she still wasn't used to its new color palette of chocolate, aubergine, olives, and lavenders. Nor was she used to its interior designer, her dad's latest girlfriend, Ingrid. Or Sigrid. Or what was that girl from Abba's name, Signifrid? At least, Courtney noted, girlfriend du jour had not futzed with the original oils her dad had commissioned of famous old-time New York baseball arenas, Ebbets Field, Giants Stadium, and Yankee Stadium.

A former major leaguer himself, Dan "Slider" Bryant had made his first million buying sports franchises and parlaying them into a vast fortune, and his dream, the sports-themed Delmonico Hotel and Casino. Which he was devoted to, nearly as much as he was to his only child, Courtney Robinson Bryant.

Flipping his cell phone closed, he smiled at her. Even at sixty, he was as physically fit as the athlete he'd once been, and drop-dead handsome—or so she was constantly told. At least once a day some woman would ask her, "How is your *gorgeous* father?" Even she had to admit that there was something kind of George Clooney about him. Why her mom had split from someone so handsome, honest, rich, and decent as Dan Bryant had been *the* mystery obsession of her childhood. It'd been superceded, in recent years, by other, more pressing obsessions. Like the one she'd come specifically to talk about.

"Did Taryn go home?" Dan asked, stretching his legs out atop his desk.

Courtney nodded as she settled into a striped overstuffed chair.

"I heard the TV on this afternoon and thought it was you so I went to check. She looked terrible," he recalled. "Was she sick?"

"Trashed," Courtney informed him. "I figured she wouldn't be in any shape for school so I left her here to sleep." She'd always—well, almost always—been completely honest with her dad. He was cool enough not to freak. Besides, living in Vegas, there wasn't much that could shock him.

"I could smell the booze on her from across the room. Was that all that she did?" he asked.

"Pot, maybe," Courtney admitted. "She doesn't do anything harder than that." *Yet,* she added silently, deciding not to share her worries with him. Honest as they were with each other, she didn't want to risk his deciding Taryn had gone too far over the edge, and curtailing her pal's carte blanche invite at the penthouse. Or worse, informing Taryn's parents.

"I don't know, Court," Dan said. "First Reign gets herself

splashed all over the headlines, now Taryn's sleeping the day away here. What gives with you girls?"

"We're being totally age-appropriate," she said teasingly. "I learned that in my first day of Psych class."

Dan chuckled, pushed back on his chair, and rose to leave. "Dad wait," she began, "what do you know about that new waiter you called me about the other night?"

Dan looked puzzled.

She prodded his memory. "The one you called to tell me was taking the guest elevator up."

"Oh, you must mean that new kid, Jake something or other . . ."

So he did know his name. Courtney filed that bit of info away.

"Yeah. Why? Was there a problem with him?"

"No," she said quickly. No one had filled Dan in about the scuffle at the party, and she wasn't about to. Getting Jake fired was not what she had in mind. "Taryn thinks he's cute," she said to cover. "Plus we saw him at school and we were just wondering how a waiter would *get* to Brighurst."

"I guess the tips here are better than I realized," he joked.

"Dad! Seriously!"

"How would I know? Maybe his parents are loaded and they want him to work to build character or he's secretly saving to buy his billionaire dad a racing car. Bill Martin, the catering manager, hired him. I don't know more than that." Dan walked over and kissed the top of her still-wet hair. "I've got to go. If you're hungry order up the lobster thermidor from downstairs. It's the dinner special tonight in the Lakers Lounge and they tell me it's out of this world."

Courtney considered. It was *possible* that Jake was a rich kid with a job. Not that she actually knew anyone with a job. Except if you counted running charity functions and stuff.

The air conditioning made her shiver. Time to get out of her wet bikini. Crossing the room toward her own apartment down the hall, she stopped by the in-house phone and pressed the button that connected to the catering office.

"Catering. Bill Martin's office," a female voice answered.

"Hi, Tanya. It's Courtney," she said to Bill's assistant. "Listen, Dad asked me to check on someone, a new waiter named Jake something."

"Oh, yeah. Real cute? Worked your party Friday night, didn't he?"

"That's him."

"Hold on. Bill just came in. I'll see what I can find out." Courtney hung on the phone only a few seconds before Tanya came back. "All Bill knows is that his name is Jake Martinez and he's living behind the hotel in the staff quarters. Other than that, he's not sure. He said your dad has the info on him. He's the one who hired him."

"My dad hired him?" Courtney asked in disbelief. And *lied* to her?

Chapter 6

Fashionista Considers Miracle Diet

Leesa pulled open the door to the Ace of Diamonds Café at Delmonico's and held it, allowing her lunch partner to pass through ahead of her. She couldn't believe she was spending her first Saturday off after a week of school with Shelby Alexis. But she had her reasons—and wasn't it what people here in Las Vegas did on a regular basis? Dined with the devil if it would further their ends. They didn't call it Sin City for nothing.

Clearly, this year Shelby was going for a look she hoped would encourage people to mistake her for Paris Hilton. *As if,* Leesa thought with a quick roll of her eyes. Shelby wore a microscopic, yellow silk, halter-back minidress with a flounced skirt that Leesa recognized as being from Elyse Walker and a pair of leather and brocade heels that she had obviously bought at Shirise. Leesa did a quick fashion damage tabulation. A thousand-dollar outfit—not including the price tag for the new blonde superlight highlights. All this getup on a Saturday afternoon? Should she tell Shel? So "un" on so many levels she decided against it.

They followed the hostess to a booth at the back of the lavish café with its red leather booths, ornate crystal chandeliers, and etched glass mirrors. "Recognize the necklace?" Shelby asked as she slid into the booth. She held up a double strand of gold dangles entwined with crystal beads.

"There's no such thing as too much bling," Leesa remarked evasively. The necklace was pretty . . . but with that dress? Overkill much?

Shelby pouted. "You don't like it. I thought you would. It's from Glitterati Boutique right here in the mall. Isn't that the place your family owns?"

"It's one of them," Leesa agreed. She studied the necklace more closely. "I recognize it now. We just got these in. It kills—with certain outfits."

"Sure . . . now that you know it's from your boutique," Shelby teased.

Leesa smiled at her. *Could you be more irritating?* she wondered silently.

"I saw the most outrageous Gucci bag while I was there. It was the studded flap bag. It comes in ostrich, velvet, or crocodile. I can't decide if I want it in pink or green."

"Oh, yeah, that just came in, too," Leesa recalled. "It has the hardware and the bamboo handle. It's gorgeous. I'd do the green."

"Your salesgirl told me that the bag is so hot that I had to put my name on a list in order to get one," Shelby complained.

"She said I would probably have to wait at least three months for it. What good is that? The season will be over by then and next year I'll need a new bag. I told her we were tight but she got all attitudey with me and insisted there was nothing she could do."

"It's true, there is a long waiting list for that bag already," Leesa said, intentionally evasive. Now she knew what Shelby was after and why she'd phoned her this morning wanting to have lunch. She hadn't even waited to order to put her cards on the table.

It was time to get to what *she* wanted from Shelby.

"We'd better decide what we want for lunch," Leesa mentioned as she opened her menu. They perused the offerings for a moment. "What are you having?" she asked.

"Double cheeseburger with fries sounds good," Shelby replied. "Oh, and look at this. They have a seven-layer fudge cake for dessert! Count me in!"

Leesa lifted her menu higher to hide the amazed expression on her face. It was crazy! How did she do it? Shelby was rail thin! A stick! Yet at parties she planted herself next to the dip and chips for the entire evening. Although she loved her champagne, Leesa had also seen her toss back one creamy, incredibly fattening white Russian after another on several occasions. And now she was at it again—cheeseburger, fries, and cake!

The insane idea of actually consuming a lunch like that made Leesa's mouth water! Her typical food download was low-cal this and dietetic that. Salads! Salads! Salads! Sushi and sashimi to the max. And Trim Spa, baby! She drank so much bottled water she sometimes made sloshing sounds when she walked.

She put in at least an hour at the gym before school every morning, too.

Anything to beat her curves into submission! If she could melt away the pounds, make the hated fat disappear, she'd have the svelte, sophisticated, fashionable frame she craved. The one thing Shelby had that Leesa coveted.

As it was, she could be mistaken for a Las Vegas showgirl, or even a stripper! It was *not* the look she wanted. But she did get mad hungry sometimes.

She took a direct approach with Shelby. "How *do* you chow down like that and still stay so thin?"

"It just comes naturally," she answered.

"For real?" Leesa asked incredulously.

"No," Shelby told her with a laugh and a light tap on her arm. "Of course not. I was a tank until about the eighth grade. You didn't know me then."

"Then how do you do it?" Leesa pressed.

"I have a system and it's foolproof. It's a secret. Although I guess I could show you, I suppose . . ." Shelby lifted her pencil-thin, sharply arched brows in an insinuating way.

At first Leesa didn't understand her meaning, but then she got it. If she wanted to play she'd have to pay. "You know, about that Gucci bag. I could move your name to the top of the list and then you'd have it by next week."

"Would you do that?!" Shelby squealed, pretending Leesa's generosity had taken her totally by surprise. "That would be fabulous."

"I'll do it as soon as we finish lunch," Leesa promised.

"You are such an awesome friend," Shelby gushed.

"So what's your magic diet secret?" Leesa asked.

"After we eat, I'll show you," Shelby said with a confident smile. "Order whatever you want from the menu. You won't gain an ounce. Trust me."

Leesa's second stepdad had once advised her to never trust a person who said, "trust me." But this was too irresistible. When the waitress came for their orders, she requested the same thing Shelby was having including the white Russian. The waitress shot down the alcohol request, reminding them that the legal drinking age was twenty one, a fact Leesa had almost forgotten. The drinking they did at the Del was strictly in private.

"We'll have two chocolate milkshakes then," Shelby said without missing a beat.

Ordering so much food made Leesa feel wild and a little out of control.

When the burger and fries arrived, Leesa inhaled their aroma. "Dig in," Shelby advised, taking a huge messy bite out of the burger, to which she'd added ketchup. With only a moment of hesitation, Leesa joined her. Eating with such abandon was something she hadn't done since she was eleven, when her womanly curves had first kicked in, making her self-conscious and miserable. Despite the lack of alcohol, she felt drunk with pleasure.

"So have you seen that waiter from the party at school this year?" Shelby inquired, eager to gossip now that she'd successfully negotiated her priority spot on the Gucci bag list. "His name is Jake Martinez. I hear he's a total border-jumping illegal, some farmworker or stablehand. I mean right off the truck."

"So what's he doing here?" Leesa asked, savoring the crunchy fries, as only the fry-deprived can.

"Turns out he's connected—related to some Vegas hot shot, a real thousand-pound gorilla."

Leesa wasn't sure she understood. "Someone's, like, cousin or something?"

Shelby wiped the ketchup off her mouth, and went to her compact to dip into the lip gloss. Leesa almost put her hand out to stop her. Not that color! But she restrained herself. She hadn't gotten what she'd come for—yet.

Shelby continued, "I don't know what the exact relation is, just that bad boy did a bad thing, wherever he lived before. And someone's paying to keep him out of trouble."

"If someone really rich brought him to be here, that would explain what he's doing at Brighurst," Leesa realized, dunking a thick, crinkle-cut fry in a mound of ketchup. "This big wig, Mr. Ape, must be the one paying the big tab. Who's he related to?"

"Can't say," Shelby replied, sipping her milkshake.

"Come on!" Leesa urged.

Shelby dabbed the chocolate from her mouth with a cloth napkin. "I promised I wouldn't tell and I can't break trust. You know how it is."

Was this for real? Leesa wondered. If so, it was a very juicy piece of gossip. It occurred to her that maybe Courtney's faux rumor—the one she started to make everyone forget about Reign's being caught on camera—maybe wasn't really so false after all.

But Shelby could be full of it. It wouldn't be the first time she'd spread a rumor just for kicks. Sometimes she just liked to pretend she was more connected than she really was.

Leesa studied her. "At least you can tell me how you found all this out."

Shelby now shot her a look that Leesa had gotten many times before. "My mom's website. Duh."

Oh, right, everyone knew Ms. Alexis's website, Gossipmaven.com, the one that supposedly dug up choice Vegas dirt. It suddenly hit Leesa that Shelby's mom probably got her "exclusive" from the little item Courtney had planted. Which made it totally meaningless.

A busboy cleared away their empty plates, just as the waitress arrived with their seven-layer cakes. "I don't think I can eat this," Leesa said, staring dubiously at the huge slab of sweetness in front of her. "I'm just too full."

"Sure you can," Shelby insisted. "Could you bring us two caffe lattes?" she asked the waitress. "We have to wash these babies down with something."

The moment Leesa put the first forkful of heavenly cake into her mouth, all her misgivings about finishing it melted into a puddle of chocolate bliss. "There's one thing I don't get," she said to Shelby, breaking off another chunk of cake. "How do we lose weight eating like this?"

Shelby pushed her plate away, her rapacious appetite finally sated. "Come to the ladies' room with me," she said, tossing her napkin onto the table. "Where is it?"

Leesa led the way down a narrow flight of stairs. A sign at the bottom of the stairs read: THE ROYAL FLUSH LOUNGE. They stopped by a door marked with a figure of a busty woman pulling a playing card—an ace of diamonds—out of her revealing bustier top. The drawing of the overripe sexpot made

Leesa silently cringe every time she saw it. It was so crude, and too much like the image she presented to others with her luscious curves.

When they were inside, Leesa waited for Shelby to produce some miracle pill from her purse. It might be some rare herbal extract she had specially imported or something else exotic. No matter how expensive it turned out to be, Leesa would persuade her parents to pay for it. Her mother certainly owed her that much for giving her genes that produced this absurdly curvy body.

"Ready?" Shelby asked.

"Absolutely," Leesa agreed.

Shelby walked into a stall. Leesa followed. Was this stuff so illegal that they had to hide in a stall?

The next thing Leesa knew, Shelby was leaning over the open bowl. Her hand was shoved down her throat and she was making horrendous wretching sounds. Her face turned deadly white. Her skinny body trembled uncontrollably as she threw up violently.

Leesa leapt back out of the way. Her hands flew to her mouth as the smell hit her—and she wanted to make sure it was all that hit her.

Shelby heaved a few more times and then she was done. She yanked a wad of toilet paper off the roll and wiped her mouth. "Your turn," she told Leesa.

"My turn?! That's your diet secret?" Leesa asked, aghast. "Bingeing and purging?"

"Works every time," Shelby said proudly. "Just stick your fingers down your throat and up comes lunch. Not a calorie left behind."

"That's so"—Leesa could not help herself—"late nineties! I mean, bulimia? That went out with like, Winona Ryder, and any Tori Spelling after-school special. *Nobody* does bulimia anymore!"

Only . . . the smell was really getting to her, making her gag, big time. She had to get out of there! She wasn't fast enough, though. In the next second, she was holding on to the next stall as her gag reflex overtook her, causing great waves of dry heaving to wrack her body.

"That's it!" Shelby encouraged enthusiastically. "Now stick your hand down your throat. Come on! You can do it! Even if it is so last century—if it ain't broke, don't fix it!"

* * *

Leesa notched the treadmill up to six miles an hour, and began running. Maybe if she sweated really, really hard, the effects of today's lunch wouldn't show. She wished she could rewind the entire day! She'd really expected more of Shelby. Bingeing and purging, aside from being so dangerous and so over, was just . . . common. So obvious!

"I can't believe you fell for that," Reign would rag her. "You actually thought Shelby had something to teach you about becoming rail thin?"

Taryn would probably say, "She's a skank and a suck-up. A bad mash-up."

"And so dangerous." She could hear Courtney's voice in her head. Courtney, their sound, steady, and smart leader. The whole eating disorder thing had, like, consumed them: back in ninth grade! They used to play a game, listing their favorite eating disorder TV movies of all time (Lifetime had a cachet);

best bulimia books—*Wasted* and *My Sister's Bones* were total classics—amazing anorexia anecdotes. Until one of the girls in school got really sick and was toted off to a clinic. And never came back.

It was then Courtney decreed there'd be no eating disorders within their group. End of story. They'd agreed. Now, actually seeing it? She was more appalled than ever.

She kicked the treadmill up to 6.5 and ran faster.

Chapter 7

Splitsville for Golf Course Heir and Celebutante Daughter?

Reign tapped lightly on the accelerator of her hot orange Mini Cooper convertible, expertly maneuvering around a slower car on the one-way drive that wove the circumference of Red Rock Canyon. The serene, majestic state park was just twenty miles away from the frenetic chaos of the Strip. The contrast of the city's faux pyramids, volcanoes, and waterfalls with the awesomeness of what Mother Nature herself created was just one of the many wonders of the Nevada desert.

All rugged cliffs, milky white limestone set against crimson canyons, Red Rock boasted dozens of hiking trails for those who wanted their nature infusion up close and personal. The main road was dotted with several spectacular scenic view lookout spots, if you preferred nature's majesty from the comfort of your car.

The only scenery Reign del Castille had a taste for was nestled beside her in the two-seater. In her eyes, the real natural wonder was Brad Simmons, her sexy, spiky-haired significant other. His aqua Izod polo shirt, collar up, matched his magnificent eyes, and when she'd picked him up, she'd noticed his khaki shorts made his butt look adorable.

Today, Reign and Brad were headed not for one of the well-marked scenic view lookout spots, but for their own personal make-out spot, secluded, unmarked, unpaved.

When Brad had text-messaged her that morning, suggesting they spend Saturday afternoon out here, Reign's sulky mood had lifted like morning fog.

He couldn't have made his intentions any clearer. By asking to log some private time together at Red Rock, he was finally ready to get their relationship back on track. Probably, he'd admit his anger and humiliation over her *Caught in the Act* debacle. Definitely, he'd follow that with the kind of making up Reign and Brad had not been doing a lot of lately.

Brad's recent indifference had hurt and worried her, and—to be really honest?—made her feel ashamed. She hadn't even told her best friends that Brad just wasn't into her lately. He neither initiated anything, nor welcomed it when she did. His apathy had switched on every circuit of Reign's hidden insecurity panel.

As she expertly navigated the car off the main drive and onto a dirt road, she shot Brad a coy look and let her hand casually drift over to his side of the car, brushing his thigh ever so lightly.

Brad removed it. "You should keep your eyes on the road," he said softly.

"I'm multitasking, baby," she purred, "just being affectionate, that's all."

He didn't answer, but turned away, to look out the window.

Do. Not. Freak. She told herself that as soon as they got to the specific spot she'd chosen, he'd be all over her. He couldn't help noticing what she'd worn, low-cut capris, and an easy-to-untie short little bolero top.

Reign slowed down, though she knew her destination by heart. The road, little more than a trail now, ended in a clearing situated by the mouth of a cozy cave.

"Look familiar?" She turned to Brad, sure he'd remember the scene of their very first time together.

He didn't.

Boys were like that, she thought, working harder to still her jumpy nerves. Reign would just have to remind him. It'd been nothing short of magical, that night they'd met, and especially later that night.

She'd been a sophomore at Brighurst, and because of her family, and friends, well known, well heeled, well connected. And epically insecure. At fifteen, the little experience Reign had with guys had done nothing to boost her confidence.

Every guy she'd gone out with had one thing in mind. It wasn't hooking up with her, it was meeting and—in their wildest teenage boy fantasies!—hooking up with her mother, the scorchingly hot Lola Marquez. Like Lola was ever even *home,* let alone open to meeting one of Reign's pubescent dates. Word spread swiftly through the Brighurst halls. A date with Reign did not get you an all-access pass to Lola's doorstep. Understandably, Reign had grown wary of guys, sure a real relationship would elude her until she was old enough to move away, and out from under the del Castille shadow.

And then Brad came along.

Brad Simmons had been a senior at Brighurst back then, a dimpled cocksure charmer with a rep for getting exactly what, and whom, he wanted. In his alligator Gucci loafers, he strutted the halls of the academy as if he owned it. And, dude, as Taryn put it, with all the money his family donated to the school, it was entirely possible that he did.

Even though he got bored easily, never stayed with one girl for too long, Brad was a catch, and if you were lucky enough to be beckoned, only the odd girl out turned the other way.

Reign surely would not have. She was equally sure she'd never get the chance. Aside from her famous family, what did she really bring to the table? In the looks, smarts, style, and personality competition, nearly every girl at Brighurst had her beat. She'd never have Courtney's slender grace, Leesa's lush curves, and certainly not Taryn's taut and tiny bod.

It'd been at the wildest party of sophomore year, Brighurst's yearly April Fool's Fiesta. Held at the estate of one of the seniors—Reign didn't even remember who—it'd gotten off the hook quickly. Alcohol was consumed prodigiously; inhibitions discarded, tequila shots had been followed by body shots. Talk about a mixer!

Reign had hung back, ostensibly because back then she could never envision herself doing anything that might, if it got out, embarrass her parents. But mainly, her insecurity over being chubby, flat-chested, and unpretty prevented her from joining in the debauchery.

She'd heard Brad was at the party, but hadn't seen him. Until he'd materialized, right next to her, nudged her elbow, and said, "Let's get out of here."

Five words had been all it took to send her heart racing, and that elbow nudge, combined with a wink of those hazel eyes and a mischievous smile, had banished her insecurities. From the jump, Brad had made her feel sexy, desirable, worthy.

She'd been a little high on a few beers, but stone-cold sober, she'd have gone with him. That night he'd driven right to this spot. (She'd refused to consider how he found it so easily or how many other times he'd brought girls here.) The car engine wasn't even shut before he had climbed on top of her.

It'd been Reign's first time having full-out sex.

It was over quickly. But afterward, he had thanked her and gently kissed her—her breasts, throat, neck, and face. This wasn't the rad Brad the school knew, the strutting I-can-get-anyone-I-want prince of his class. This was, she decided then and there, the real Brad, private, tender, humble, grateful and not afraid to show it. That was the moment Reign del Castille had fallen in love with him. That's what it was, too, no matter what she'd told Dr. Sullivan.

Even now one and a half on-again, off-again years later, the only time she ever saw that sweet side of Brad was immediately after they had sex. And so, even though his lead-in remained artlessly abrupt, she lived for the worshipful gaze and tender kisses he bestowed on her afterward.

Now, Reign turned off the engine, hoping to turn Brad on as she had for most of their time together. "Want to go for a walk?" she suggested, motioning toward the mouth of the cave. "I brought a soft lambskin blanket." She winked at him, and let her hand graze on his thigh again.

"Not so much, not now," he declined.

Her eyes widened in surprise as she tried to quell her rising panic. No way had he brought her to Red Rock to what . . . break up with her? And then she remembered: he probably wanted to talk about the *Caught in the Act* thing. She should probably be acting more contrite and less horny. The next words out of his mouth confirmed it.

"Look, I wanted to come here because it's private and I need to ask you something really personal," he told her, squirming just a bit.

Reign unintentionally leaned closer to him, eagerly anticipating what he would say next, how he'd put it exactly. Was he more ticked about the publicity, or just her and Oliver? Would he say that he'd changed his mind about their relationship? That he did care what she did out of town, and didn't want her hooking up with Oliver or anyone else when she was away from him?

She considered her response. The meaningless out-of-town tumbles gave her a rush, excitement . . . and control. If Brad asked her to stop? It wasn't even a question. Deep inside, Reign knew she'd do anything he asked.

No matter what.

"I need to borrow some money."

Her mouth fell open. Nausea threatened to overtake her. "Whaaat?"

"This isn't easy for me to talk about," he assured her.

"And yet, it looks like you're about to," she said, a little more sharply than she would've liked.

His eyes darted around, as if he could, and would, look at anything but her. "I just don't know how things got to this point. But I need to borrow eighteen thousand dollars."

"Eighteen thousand . . ." She trailed off, "This is why we're here?"

"If you could lend me seventeen thou, I could probably scrape together the rest," he allowed.

She leaned against the car door, staring at him incredulously. Slowly her shock dissipated; reason returned. "What do you need money for? And why can't you just ask your father for it?"

"I can't tell him I racked up nearly twenty g's in gambling debt!" he cried, raking his hair miserably so that it became more Ryan Cabrera than Ty Pennington. "He doesn't even know I play poker. He's always saying it's a sucker's game. He'd lose all respect for me."

"But he *would* give you the money, right?" Reign pressed.

A bitter grin twisted Brad's formerly sweet face. "He'd cough up the funds fast if he knew whom I owed it to," he said ominously, "but I'd do anything so he never finds out about it."

Her stomach clenched. "Who do you owe the money to?"

"Look, Reign, you know I've been on a losing streak lately. It'll end, they always do. But in the meantime, I didn't want the guys I play with to think I was a stiff, so I went to a shark for the cash."

"A shark?" Reign repeated dumbly.

"A loan shark. A guy named Theodore. He gives you the cash, no questions asked, but he charges you interest."

"Oh, like a credit card?" she asked hopefully. That didn't seem so scary. That kind of debt she understood.

"Sort of. Except the interest rate is higher—and if you don't pay? . . . it's not like they put you on a payment schedule, or cut up your card," Brad said bitterly. "He sends his guys out to seriously mess you up."

"What do they do?" Reign was trembling.

He turned away. A slight catch in his voice betrayed the fear he'd tried to mask with a matter-of-fact manner. "They're arm breakers. You know. They beat the shit out of you and if they go too far, accidentally do more damage, it's like, like, oh, well."

She stared at him as he gazed out the window morosely. She'd never seen him so vulnerable, so terrified. Brad exuded confidence, control. This shark thing, it'd thrown him. It was probably, she reflected, the worst thing Brad had ever faced. And he'd come to her for help. He'd opened up to her.

Reign knew what she had to do.

A cash withdrawal from one of her credit cards would cover his debt and her parents' accountant would pay it, no questions asked. Besides, she could say she bid on something at some charity auction.

"Done," she told him.

He turned back to her sharply. "You can give me the cash?"

"I can lend it to you," she amended.

"Whatever. That's great! Can you get it today?"

"Monday."

Massively relieved, Brad relaxed his shoulders, closed his eyes, and whispered, "Thank you, Reign. You're a lifesaver."

Stretching, she kicked her Capri-clad legs up, swung them in his direction, and wrapped them around him. "There's no sense wasting this great view," she said seductively. "Now that business is settled, how about pleasure?"

For a moment he seemed to consider her suggestion. Then

he shook his head. "Sorry, babe. I'm not feeling it. I'm probably too tense."

Bending her legs, she swung back into driving position and started the engine. "Whatever," she said coldly, backing up the car. "Anyone might be tense if there was a chance he was going to have his perfect preppy nose broken in five places."

Scenic Drive was one-way. To return to the city, she'd have to cruise the entire loop surrounding the canyon. With her foot heavily on the gas, she sped forward, angry and humiliated by his rejection. Brad had turned to her in a weak moment; he was grateful, but he still didn't desire her.

Was he, then, after all their time together, about to be exposed as just like the others? Reign grimaced. Was he just some jerk who'd gotten close to her because of what she was—a movie star daughter with an unlimited credit card—not who she was?

Brad had always vibed on being seen with her; he'd been all about their pictures snapped for the "Pulse" section of *Las Vegas* magazine or the rival glossy *Vegas,* in their "ShotOn-Site" column, posing among the hot, young, and rich celebutantes. Along with Courtney, Leesa, and Taryn, Reign was invited to every club and/or restaurant opening. Guys who came with invariably attained their own celeb-cred.

"Slow down!" he cried as she careened around a turn. "Are you pissed at me about this?"

"You're the one with a problem lately," she shouted over the wind. "You never want to do anything anymore. At least not with me."

"Give me a break," he complained angrily. They didn't talk again until she stopped at a light on Charleston Boulevard heading back into the city. "Reign, I don't want you to be mad at me," he said in a conciliatory tone.

"Because then I might not lend you the money?" she snapped. "You don't want me, but you keep me around for the cachet—and cash—is that it?" She'd never been that verbally brutal with him before.

"Come on," he moaned. "I'm not that horny lately 'cause I have stuff on my mind. Power down the paranoia, would you?"

Paranoid? Was she? In a way she hoped so.

Pulling to a stop in front of the UNLV frat house that Brad called home, she screeched to the curb to let him out. "See ya tonight?" he said as he leapt out over the side. "The bash at New York, New York. Kevin A's birthday, remember? I'll meet you there."

Reign relented. "Could we go together?"

He sighed. "You know I can't. Have to give some guys a ride. I already committed. You know how it is."

"Yeah," she agreed curtly and angrily sped away, not even pausing to watch his butt as he walked to the house.

* * *

Reign took the long way across town to her family's estate in Summerlin. Del Castille Manor, a twelve-thousand-square-foot gothic-style mansion on its own private lake, was situated in a heavily guarded, gated enclave. She drove up the circular driveway, left the car running for the valet to deal with, and powered through the massive mahogany front doors.

Maybe she'd overreacted to Brad's dilemma. Maybe he had gotten himself into a jam and couldn't be distracted. Maybe she was being paranoid.

The party tonight would help lift her spirits . . . she was sure of it. And then there was Sunday, when she could hang with her Girls.

With a bit more swing in her step, Reign vaulted up the circular staircase and headed for her bedroom, one of seven in the manor. Her parents, she knew, were not home. This weekend both were in Hollywood, her dad just started some new Spielberg film, her mom still on her round of press events for *The Last Kiss,* her new film.

She and her sisters were under the "watchful" eyes of the del Castille staff, as they so often were. As she padded through the second floor of the house, she heard the unremarkable sounds of the flute coming from the conservatory. Her youngest sister, ten-year-old Haven, must be having a lesson with her private instructor.

Reign popped her head into Starshine's suite, found her sister lounging on the curved white couch, gossiping with someone on her cell while tossing her luxe black hair this way and that.

Both her sisters resembled their gorgeous, sexy actress mother, while she was unmistakably her father's daughter. Wavy, nearly black hair, and a broad-shouldered physique might be striking on him but they didn't translate on a chick. Courtney and Leesa were forever assuring her that she was cute, had her own style, and should work it. Leesa could help her. But Reign had resisted, refusing to let go of the fantasy that she'd soon age-out of her baby fat—grow another inch or two—wake up flawless one magic day. And if that never happened? Brad loved her just the way she was, or used to.

She examined herself in front of the gold-rimmed rectangular mirror in the hallway. If she wanted to know why Brad wasn't that into her she didn't have to look much further than here, she thought miserably.

"Everything all right, ducky?" asked Ginger, Haven's tall, gorgeous British nanny asked as she walked past.

"Right as Reign," she joked mirthlessly.

"Why don't you go down to the spa? A little soak in the Jacuzzi and a massage will perk you up," she suggested.

Reign regarded the attractive young woman. She liked Ginger, who often acted like a big sister to her. Reign never appreciated it more than at that moment. At least someone was simply being kind to her—without wanting anything from her.

"You might want to get them to do your makeup and blow-dry your hair while you're down there," Ginger added. "Your mom and dad called. They want you and your sisters to fly out to Hollywood tonight for a photo shoot with them tomorrow. You'll be taking the jet out of McClarren to LAX at six."

"No way! I have a party to go to!" she objected.

Ginger shrugged helplessly. "They told me to have you girls there, good to go. Your mom more or less implied that my job depends on it."

Reign shook her head with bitter resignation. The momentary gratitude she'd felt toward Ginger evaporated into an acid mist. The woman didn't care about her—she was just doing her job. How stupid she'd been to think that Ginger was different from anyone else.

Chapter 8

Punk Princess Reamed by Classical Pops!

Taryn bounced on the antique Louis XIV silk brocade couch as if it were a trampoline, playing air guitar to the new, as yet unreleased, Bones bonus track. She'd downloaded it illegally, burned it onto a CD mix, and was now blasting the music, shouting the lyrics right over lead singer Fury's manic growl.

Cool beans! This time it was gonna happen: she could feel it—she giggled, stopping to catch a whiff of weed from the roach in the ashtray—in her bones!

The Bones were coming to Delmonico's.

The owner of the Del? Courtney Bryant's dad.

Courtney Bryant? Her girl, her homie, her best friend.

Even she, arithmetically challenged and proud of it, could do *that* kind of math.

She had to make Courtney promise, pinky-swear, to actually *get* her the all-access pass to the Bones' backstage party, and the after-event in the guest penthouse. That was where she and Fury would direct-connect. And *score!* He'd hear Taryn's music, and an instant and unbreakable bond would form. United forever in their passion for screamo rock, the ultimate mash-up of metal and emo. The music that came from her soul.

Courtney had promised to "do what she could." Which should've translated to: done deal. Dude, what *couldn't* Courtney pull off in Vegas? So what up with the cagey crap sista-friend was pulling? The concert was comin' up soon. Courtney should have produced that backstage pass by—

"Now!"

Taryn twirled, midbounce—mouth agape at the rangy, silver-haired man who'd suddenly materialized in the living room.

"Now! Shut that noise off!" he thundered, his patrician face a portrait in rage.

"Pops? You're . . . you're . . . here?" Taryn sputtered.

"That would be the obvious," Ivan Krakowski said sternly, stalking up to the killer Bose speaker system, hitting the eject button, and yanking the CD out of its compartment.

Taryn did her best chagrined smile. "I wasn't actually expecting you until later."

"Again with the obvious," her father scolded. "Tell me something I don't know."

Taryn leapt off the couch and flung her arms around her father's waist. She hugged him hard. There was no better way to defuse a fuming father than play Daddy's Little Girl. Especially when, well, she kinda *was* Daddy's little girl.

In spite of their myriad differences of opinion. In spite of the fact that he was the most famous conductor the Las Vegas Symphony ever had. And she was hoping to be the most famously vicious punk rocker to ever come out of Vegas.

"What have I told you," he continued, trying to remain righteously enraged, "about bringing this garbage into the house?"

He absolutely despised the music Taryn loved.

She looked up at him, wishing she'd inherited even a fraction of his commanding height. An unruly shock of his silver-white hair fell into his eyes as it sometimes did when he was in the throes of conducting an orchestra in a particularly passionate, soaring piece of music he'd composed.

Or like now, when he was passionately pissed off—or trying to be!

Taryn was reminded of an old album cover framed on the wall in his den: *Ivan Krakowski Conducts!* The cover photo, a classic, captured him with his conductor's baton raised dramatically, eyes fiery, and with that same lock of hair—only it was brown back then—having fallen over his eye.

"You look cute, Pops," she cooed at him.

He harrumphed. "I walk in the front door after being away for a week, on a long, hard concert engagement, and discover my daughter screeching scatological idiocies and destroying the furniture."

Taryn cut her eyes toward the heinous couch, which unfortunately had easily withstood her manic moves.

"I know the Bones aren't your thing, but I didn't think anyone was home," she started to explain.

"So if I'm not home, that makes it all right?" he challenged.

She shrugged.

Ivan Krakowski sighed, the steam out of him now. He let Taryn lead him over to the couch. "Want me to get you some tea?" she offered.

He leaned back and closed his heavily lidded eyes. "That would be nice."

She scurried up and hit the intercom, instructing the housekeeper, Mavis, in exactly what kind of herbal tea best soothed her tired, grouchy pops. "And bring me the same, if you don't mind," Taryn said politely.

"I know what you're doing," Ivan said steadily. "It's all well and good to butter me up, but we're talking about your future here. And if you insist on filling your head, and this house, with that kind of . . ." He paused and shook his head. "I refuse to call it music. And those lyrics—disgusting!"

So he *had* been listening, standing there longer than she'd realized. "The Bones need strong words, Pops. You can't take on global corruption with nice, polite lyrics."

"Strong words don't need to be obscene," he argued.

"Pops, you're a musician. An artist! Of all people, you can't condone censorship. It says so in the Philharmonic Handbook for Dummies."

If he appreciated the joke, he didn't let on. "That's where you're wrong, my darling. I can, and do, censor from you the Broken Bones, or whatever you call them. This kind of junk will not make the admissions committee at Juilliard happy."

Right on. The *last* thing she wanted to do was make the stuck-up Juilliard admissions committee happy. She wanted to make them so unhappy, no way would they accept her. Legend or no legend. Daughter of Ivan Krakowski or daughter of Ivan the Terrible.

She knew him well enough not to *say* any of that.

He knew her well enough to know exactly what she was thinking. "I won't sit around watching you sabotage your future . . ."

Here comes the soliloquy.

"Do you really want to waste your talent so cavalierly on some—some—youthful rebellion that will be over just like this?" He snapped his fingers in the air. "You realize, I hope, that when this adolescent phase passes, you will have utterly squandered your chance at a musical career. The time to study and make a name for yourself is now. You can never recapture it. And furthermore, if you think I can't smell the marijuana in this room . . ."

She needed neither to hear nor to heed his words. She knew them by heart.

Her father spoke passionately, with complete conviction. His assuredness was absolute. It shook her to the core.

A million snappy answers sprang into her mind but stuck in her throat. Her father was so strong-minded, had such a powerful charisma in his own dignified fashion, that he wasn't someone she could defy openly for long, especially when he was deadly serious, as he was now. It was his deeply held conviction that she was a gifted violinist and pianist, and it hurt her that he was so disappointed that she did not share his love of classical music.

"I want to play rock guitar," she said, despising the meekness in her voice.

He pressed on, "You have a gift. We don't *ask* for our gifts. But when they are bestowed upon us, we have a responsibility to develop them, to share them, not to waste them."

She was reminded of that line from *Spider-Man*: "With great power comes great responsibility." Yeah, well, with great gifts comes a lot of shit.

Why couldn't he see that just because she chose to bestow her gifts on the young, the disenfranchised, the angry—that was as important as the la-di-da classical gasbags he played for?

"You will go to Juilliard in the fall. You will become the great classical violinist and musician you are destined to be. End of story."

Taryn felt her stomach sinking.

Mavis arrived with their tea. She'd added scones for Ivan and homemade s'mores for her. Mavis was so devoted to their family, she always intuited exactly what was needed.

Ivan noticed the faded bruise across her cheek for the first time. "What happened to your face?" he asked brusquely, as though he suspected that somehow she'd brought this on herself.

She told him the same lie she'd told her mother Tuesday evening when she'd finally gotten home. "I slipped in school and smacked right into a locker. They have that weird marble in the hallways that gets so slippery when it's wet. Somebody must have spilled something."

Her mother had bought it, letting the subject pass with an inane reprimand about watching where she was going.

Her father scrutinized her more closely than her mother had, lifting her chin and turning her heart-shaped face from side to side. "Does it hurt if you touch it?"

"No."

"All right. There's probably no broken bone then. And

probably no point in asking how you really got it." With that, he sipped his tea, pinky in the air.

She did the same.

Yes, father and daughter loved each other. And that was the damn of it. She didn't let him see the tears welling in her eyes.

* * *

"Reign's depressed, we've got to do something." The text message from Leesa had been one of several similarly themed messages waiting on Taryn's cell phone.

"Brad's being a jerk and she's in deep depression," Courtney confided.

Leesa typed. "She's beating herself up, like she's the reason *he's* an axxx-hole. She's totally on a downward spiral."

"Intervention required," Courtney had written. "Let's cut out of school early on Monday and take her to the spa."

Leesa was all over it. "A massage, an eyebrow pluck, definitely a waxing. That'll do wonders for her self-esteem."

Yeah, that'll work, thought Taryn sarcastically. She texted her friends back: "Reign doesn't need a waxing. She needs surgery to remove Brad, and then, an extreme Zoloft makeover."

* * *

Knowing they were only doing a half-day made Monday at Brighurst less sucky. Taryn decided to decorate her already fading bruise, art it up. Working with Courtney's stylist, she'd opted for thick black liner, heavy mascara, and then ultravibrant blue, purple, turquoise, and green eye shadows. She drew them in feathering strokes, up to her brows, down to her cheekbones, and out to her ears. She looked like a punk peacock.

Excellent!

Her wardrobe went with. Today she wore her spiked choker, ripped fishnet arm warmers, black nail polish, and her biggest studded Frye boots. The total effect? The future lead guitarist for the Bones, the first woman Fury would invite into the band. It was only a matter of time.

"It's the zombie queen of hard rock," Reign teased her that afternoon when she joined her pals for lunch. They were in the sunny courtyard poking at their ordered-in sushi with chopsticks. "Are you sure the sun won't melt your undead skin?"

"I hope not, at least not until I can bite Fury's neck and make him my undead sex slave," she cracked, taking her seat with them.

"You are a psycho," Leesa commented, shaking her head.

"A psycho with a dream," Taryn quipped, shooting a look at Courtney. "And a friend who can make that dream come true. Yet, won't."

Courtney did a "not that again" sigh.

"The Bones concert is, like, three weeks away and you haven't secured me the all-access pass. Can we sidebar away from Reign's ignoble behavior to deal with what is that about?"

Courtney folded her arms. "I said I was trying to get you the pass."

"Courtney Bryant doesn't need to try," Taryn challenged. "She either does it or doesn't. You've got the *pow*-uh," she sing-songed.

"Look, I . . ." Courtney's eyes darted around nervously. "I'm not sure it's the best idea. For you."

Taryn felt like she'd been sucker-punched. "So what you're saying is you don't think my music is good enough, you don't think *I'm* good enough to gain entrée to the Bones' backstage party. You think Fury will kick my sorry ass right outta there. And you don't want that happening at your hotel. Does that about sum it up?"

"No!" Courtney recoiled. "I don't think that at all. How could you say that?"

"I just did," Taryn growled.

Courtney pressed her lips together in a tight line. "Listen to me, Taryn. I've known you forever. I respect and love you. As for your music? You're a prodigy, a genius! Everyone knows that. It's about your . . . well, it's about your safety. They have a rep . . ."

A wide smile spread across Taryn's lips. "Is that all? Sista-friend, I can so take care of myself. I promise. You get me the pass. You'll see—that, and more."

"That's what I'm afraid of," murmured Courtney.

"I heard that," Taryn warned her. "Now, back to our regularly scheduled dramas. How churns the rumor mill? Is anyone still riveted by our 'not who he claims to be' item?"

"It's fading," Courtney admitted, looking concerned. "We have to somehow feed the fire or it's going to die. Or worse, stand by while Reign gets 'Caught In The Act' again."

Reign tsk-tsked. "Instead of going to Randy's party on Sunday, like I was supposed to . . ." She paused for sympathy effect. "I made my own fun. I hooked up with the assistant of the photog who did the shoot in L.A. This gorgeous Asian guy. Don't worry, no stalkerazzi, no one will know."

"You'd better hope so," Courtney said. "Still, I really have to pump up that rumor. Has anyone heard anything more about Jake Martinez?"

They shook their heads. "Zilch," Taryn said, wondering why Courtney was focusing on that waiter guy. Surely, there were other candidates at Brighurst way riper for serious gossip.

"Talk to people," Courtney suggested. "Something's got to be up with him."

"Maybe he's on a scholarship," Reign offered.

"Maybe—but that's hardly buzz-worthy. Who'd care, really?" She paused, "But still, I wish we could find out for sure."

Bet you do, Taryn mused. After lunch, Taryn got a slight reefer buzz on and floated through her classes dreaming about Fury. Who knew? Maybe after he fell for her music, he'd fall for her. When she arrived at English, the last class she'd be attending that day, her teacher handed her a note.

Please have Taryn report to the dean's office immediately.

So, she thought, prancing out of English, the bright lights at Brighurst finally realized she'd been AWOL Monday and Tuesday three weeks ago!

It wasn't a huge deal. If they tried to inform her parents, she'd simply intercept the phone message, the email, or the letter home before it fell into Mynda or Ivan's hands—even if she had to cut out early to do it. Her mother never turned on her cell phone, using it only for calls out, and her father was so old school he didn't have one at all. (In fact, he loathed them with an almost frightening hatred because they were forever ringing at some quiet, dramatic moment of his concerts, utterly destroying the moment.)

"Hello, Miss Krakowski," one of the three Brighurst secretaries greeted her with neutral politeness when she entered the main office. "Dean Temple would like to see you." She ushered Taryn into the small office of Susan Temple, dean of seniors from A through M.

Taryn sat. Dean Temple would lecture her about making this year count, reminding her about her college applications, and give her forms for her parents to sign. They always started out easy in the beginning of the year, not coming down too hard for the first four cuts or so.

As she waited for the dean to show up, she noticed that one of the tall filing cabinets lining the room was unlocked and ever so slightly open. It was marked K-M—since her own file was already on the desk, Dean Temple had obviously forgotten to close the drawer.

Stealthily, she got up, walked over to the open file cabinet, and began quickly thumbing through. She had it. Jake Martinez! Grabbing the manila file, she slipped it into the middle of her tote just as Susan Temple walked in the door.

Chapter 9

Party Girls Do Wellness Intervention

The spa at the Delmonico outluxuriated every other such resort facility in Vegas in every way—aesthetically, exotically, and quasi-erotically; that is, clients were ministered to by the hottest licensed therapists and masseurs on the planet. Dan Bryant had poured megamillions into it, on Courtney's assurance that to retain their rep as the single most happening hotel for hipsters, hip-hoppers, athletes, and A-listers—you needed a kick-ass spa. Duh.

Against a backdrop of white onyx floors, slate, frosted glass, and rainfall corridors, SpaMonico was sixty-five thousand square feet of pure pampering space. It was total Zen *and* total Vegas, an environment created to imitate the real thing: a state of mind meant to refresh mind, body, and spirit. And this afternoon, Courtney could think of no one whose mind, body, and spirit needed more rebooting, whose self-esteem needed more boosting, than that of Reign del Castille.

The girls had limoed straight over from their sixth-period classes, and were soon wrapped in luxe Frette robes (sold in the spa gift store, owned by Leesa's parents), their tootsies in soft slippers, and treated to a candlelit aromatherapy area, where they snacked on fresh fruit slices and purified water. The concept of curing-by-spa was Courtney's, but Leesa took over the actual assignment of treatments. She knew what her girls needed most. A quick dip in the plunge pools, four-by-eight-foot tubs filled with sweet-smelling rosebuds and customized essential oils and accented by loofahs and pillows, to be followed by customized treatments.

Now, three of them were belly-flopped on massage tables situated so that they could face each other, as their bodies were being stroked, pummeled, and worked by Eduardo, Ti-hwa, Dennis, and Javier, one sexier than the next. A fact not unappreciated by any of them.

For Courtney, Leesa had suggested an Egyptian gold body treatment. "It's inspired by the beauty rituals of ancient Egypt," she explained. "You get exfoliated, wrapped in oils and lotions, rinsed off, and finally dusted with gold powder."

"Sounds . . . sparkly," Courtney commented warily. She wasn't so much the sparkle fan.

"You do have a date with Liam later tonight, do you not?" Leesa reminded her.

"At eight," Courtney replied.

"Well, don't you want to shimmer for him? If I had someone like him, I would!" Leesa exclaimed.

Courtney laughed, loving Leesa at that moment. "I'll see if I can clone him."

For a second, Courtney thought Leesa actually believed . . . no. Not going there.

Taryn opted for the toughest treatment available. "The one where the dude stomps on your back," as she'd indelicately put it.

"It's called Ashiatsu Oriental Bar Therapy," Leesa informed her, "and the 'dude' is Ti-hwa Tseng, a licensed barefoot masseur who will walk on your back. It's intense, a really deep massage, and mostly men have it."

"Bring it," was Taryn's response.

She herself was on a mat on the floor just beneath her friends. Leesa wanted to do Thai yoga, a combination of acupressure, energy balancing, stretching, and yoga exercise. Later, she'd do the Caviar Fusion Facial.

Reign, whose face was wrapped in a cinnamon mud mask, was getting the Fleur Garden Aromatherapy treatment, being rubbed and wrapped in floral oils for ultimate hydrating. In Leesa's experience, hydrating was the holy grail of wellness. To feel better about yourself, one's body needed water.

"I'm fat and ugly," Reign groused.

"Rub more oils on her," Leesa instructed, head between her knees, tush upon the air, from her downward dog position.

Courtney countered, "She doesn't need more oils—she needs to unload, tell us why she's feeling so crappy. Reign, honey, what's wrong?"

"He doesn't want to touch me," Reign finally admitted, "and he doesn't want me touching him. In any way. I'm repulsive."

"Whoa. Down, girl," Taryn said. "There's a quota on self-evisceration, and you're getting close."

Leesa thought for a moment. "So you mean Brad doesn't want to have sex with you?"

"Not in weeks," Reign said woefully.

"Not from you," Taryn pointed out.

The only sound in the room was the crack of the barefoot masseur walking on Taryn's back.

"Is he, like, upset about something?" Leesa asked. "Maybe about those other guys you've been with?"

"I dunno, maybe," Reign mumbled.

"Gambling issues?" Courtney guessed.

"No!" Reign refuted, a little too forcefully.

"Even if he was freaked about something else, name me one dude who doesn't want to get it on. It's sexual healing— that classic Marvin Gaye song had it right," Taryn put in. "As for other guys? You'd think that'd make him even hornier, make him want to prove he's the alpha male in Reign's life."

"Maybe he's sick or something," Leesa speculated.

"Sick of me," Reign moaned.

"Well," Taryn managed, "that can only mean one thing. He's hooking up with someone else."

"He can't be. Here? In Vegas? That's against the rules," Reign pointed out. "We don't do that."

"Maybe *you* don't . . ."

"No way," Leesa, doing a tiger stretch, said between clenched teeth, "Brad may not always be the nicest, but he's not a betrayer. He wouldn't do that to you."

"Yeah, he would," Taryn countered. "He's slimier than your oil-soaked tummy right now."

"Taryn!" Courtney could feel herself tensing, in spite of

Dennis's magic thumbs working her shoulders. "You're so not helping."

Reign lifted her chin off the massage table. "You believe that, don't you, Courtney? I can hear it in your voice. You think Brad's got a bimbo stashed somewhere . . . here?"

"Well, not in this room," Taryn joked, "although I didn't scour in the bottom of the pool—maybe we should send a search and rescue scuba team . . ."

"Taryn! It's not funny!" Leesa scolded.

Courtney interrupted, "That's not what I said. I'm just saying that if you're getting a weird vibe from Brad, it means something; you're not crazy—or fat or repulsive. Something's definitely going on, but it's not necessarily about you. Boys sometimes have, you know, performance anxiety, if they're freaked out about something else. In his case, I'd guess money."

Reign paled. Not an easy thing to do behind her cinnamon mud mask. "Brad doesn't have money issues."

Courtney knew the hollow sound of a lie when she heard one.

Chapter 10

Courtney Goes One-on-One with Mystery Boy!

Student's Full Name: Jacob Pino Martinez
Application for entry into Brighurst Academy: Approved August 21
Status: Senior
Tuition: Paid in full for year

In the far corner of the airy, cavernous library/media center of Brighurst Academy, blocked by tall stacks of books and computer stations, Courtney snuggled into a large, comfy club chair. On her lap, should anyone nose by, an oversized edition of Shakespearean sonnets. But it wasn't the wherefor-art-thou-Romeo scene she was reading, nor Lady Macbeth's soliloquy, nor poor Yorick's end. It was the chapter and verse tucked inside the big Bard volume that captivated her attention.

The official Brighurst file on Jake Martinez.

It made for spellbinding reading. And gave her a real reason to stay on campus after school, something she rarely if ever did. Only one of her Girls knew the real reason she'd begged off their shopping recon trip to the Bellagio.

Taryn. That little sneak. That little blackmailing bundle of balls-out nerve. Courtney could've kissed her! Even if the little schemer had waited until after the spa intervention to reveal her masterstroke of cunning—that she'd stolen Jake's official school file! And even if she'd held it for ransom.

Until Courtney solemnly swore, on Liam's life *or* that new Hermès bag, whichever she held more sacred, to procure that Bones backstage pass and after-party VIP badge. Until such time, according to Taryn, Courtney wasn't even getting a peek at that file.

It'd taken Courtney less than a millisecond to cave to Taryn's demands.

It'd been worth it. The info dump on Jake was stunning. Oh, there was dirt here: most fascinating. But more frustrating. Because as much as the file exposed about him, it omitted more.

Courtney craved a full reveal on Jake, to find a reason why she cared so damn much. Once she unraveled that personal little knot, she'd be home free: that is, free of this ridiculous obsession. Back to her real life, which in the boy category had room for only one person. Which ought to be Liam. The extremely hot, appropriate, perfect-match Liam.

So why the reckless infatuation with this kid?

Maybe the answer was in the paperwork.

Jake was born in Los Angeles, at St. John's Hospital. He grew up in El Segundo and East L.A., where he'd gone to public high school. The abrupt transfer to pricey, posh Brighurst in his senior year was only one of the head-scratchers in his file. Why move in your senior year? Unless you got some amazing scholarship, or one of your parents had gotten a job in Las Vegas, along with a hefty raise. There was no mention of either in the file.

His mother, in fact, one Rosa Martinez, was deceased. It didn't say when she'd died. But since there was no other mention of a guardian, or other relatives, Courtney calculated that it'd been recent. But how recent? And where was dear old dad in the picture?

The space for "Father's Name" was maddeningly blank. Which meant one of three things:

The mother didn't know who the father was.

The mother was claiming immaculate conception.

The father was some serious big shot who'd paid not to have his name on the school records.

Her gut said the answer was behind door number three. The mystery dad was a powerful hot shot, or related to one. Someone was paying Jake's full tuition at Brighurst.

Courtney continued to scan the file. All his school records were there, from kindergarten on up. Jake had done well academically—but not so well behaviorally. She stifled a guffaw. His record for detention would make Taryn proud! His birthday was listed as November 20. He'd turn eighteen in two months, just like her. That made them both Scorpio—vain, charismatic, proud, potentially treacherous, quick to anger, sexually magnetic. Or would two Scorpios repel each other? She wondered . . .

The paperwork confirmed that Jake did, indeed, bunk in

the Delmonico staff quarters behind the hotel, but only gave a post office box in Las Vegas as a billing address. It gave his class schedule, which Courtney jotted down. Not because she wanted to, like, stalk him or anything. She was all about intel.

Another question burned, licking at the corners of her mind. Her father lied to her about hiring Jake. She'd never known him to lie before. Which meant it had to be something really serious. Courtney didn't scare easily, but heading down that road was not a place she dared go.

"It's five o'clock, Courtney, the library's closing," a library aide softly told her as she pushed a book cart past her.

It was? She hadn't realized how long she'd lingered over the file. She'd told her Girls she'd catch up with them around five—she needed some accessories for her dinner with Liam at eight-thirty.

Courtney nodded and closed the huge volume in front of her, but not before surreptitiously slipping Jake's file into her powder blue Balenciaga bag. She was about to call Leesa to tell her she'd be late, but decided to buzz Delmonico's and order up a limo to bring her home. It'd take a good twenty minutes, she was told, since rush hour had begun.

Best use of her waiting time? Returning the file to Dean Temple's office. She had it committed to memory anyway, and the longer it went missing, the sooner they might finger Taryn for the culprit. Taryn hardly needed more trouble.

The clickity-click of her stiletto heels on the school's polished marble floors was going to make a stealth visit to the dean's office impossible. Courtney needed a pit stop at her locker to change into her Pumas. For a split second she realized how ridiculous she looked, a Stella McCartney sundress with sneakers! All she needed were white socks to finish the laughably ridiculous "commuter" look. But no one would see her, so it didn't really count.

It was between the locker and the dean's office that she passed the window overlooking Brighurst's athletic fields.

Her heart leapt into her throat.

There was a lone figure on the basketball court, shooting one basket after another.

She squinted into the late afternoon sun, mesmerized by the repetitive thud of the ball against the backboard, and by the hoopster himself. Dark glossy hair, too long for any self-respecting male Brig-prig, grubby hi-tops, sagged-out jeans, and a T-shirt. A T-shirt that clung to his lat muscles and turned her legs to jelly. Any thoughts of returning his file disappeared like quarters in a slot machine.

There was no question, she had to go out there.

If he sensed her presence, he played it cool, shooting several more baskets before turning in her direction. He didn't act surprised to see her.

"Hey" was all he said before turning back to his solo game.

Fighting to slow her speeding heart, desperate to seem cool, she silently scolded herself, *Just breathe.* Some force, powerful and completely outside of herself, made her walk right over to him.

"It's late, past five," she reported, wanting to kill herself. Could that have been any lamer?

He wiped a light mist of sweat from his forehead with the sleeve of his T-shirt. "Thanks for the time-check. What are you doing here? After-school project?"

"You could say that," she replied, wondering how he'd

react if she told him the details of the project that'd kept her on campus. "I was in the library."

"You were? What could possibly be in the school library that you couldn't access from your private penthouse?"

The sarcasm irked her. "I don't know you," she said snippily, "and I don't appreciate your attitude."

"So what are you gonna do, have me fired?" The twinkle in his dark eyes threw her.

"Maybe I will."

"Maybe you should."

This was ridiculous! Courtney tried to turn regally on her heel. Except she was wearing Pumas, which so didn't have the same effect. Suddenly, a wild thought hit her and she spun around.

"I can kick your butt in this game." She motioned toward the basketball hoop.

He arched his eyebrows in surprise. "You're suggesting one-on-one?"

"If you dare."

A sly smile spread across his full lips just then, and the sun caught his wide flat cheekbones. He tossed her the ball. "Knock yourself out, Rebecca Lobo."

Courtney was a superior player. Her height and natural athletic ability had been honed by countless hours playing hoops with her father. It was the primary way the former professional athlete relaxed, and over the years, a place for Dan and Courtney to bond. She'd never do anything so pathetic as join the girls' team at school, but that didn't mean she couldn't have been their star player.

She dribbled, and then drove hard toward the basket, while

he guarded her. Concentrating proved challenging. Jake's smooth cocoa-butter skin distracted her, his taut, ropy muscles fought for her attention, she kept stealing glances at his piercing, dancing eyes. Unsurprisingly, Courtney fumbled her first few attempts—but the realization that Jake was trouncing her kick-started her natural competitive streak. Soon, a respectable game was under way.

He caught the ball and bounced it several times before shooting. It circled the rim then fell in. She scooped it up from underneath and took a quick inside shot that fell in cleanly.

After a while, they hit their stride, getting into a rhythm, and Courtney began to relax. "So, how do you like Brighurst?" she asked.

Without pause, he shot back, "Implying there's something to like about *Prig*hurst? I hate every second of it."

"Tell us what you really think," she managed to quip, decisively sinking a basket.

"Good one!" he complimented her. "This school is like Camp Cupcake, a country club for pampered brats paid for by their powerful parents. It's full of stuck-up snobs who have it made, and know it."

So why are *you* here? is what she wanted to ask, but didn't. Nor did he offer it up. Alt thought: Did she really want to know?

"Do you like working at the Del? I mean . . . as a waiter?"

He laughed. "Why? If I don't, can you hook me up with a better gig? Maybe I could be a casino boss. Or a pimp—"

She shoved the ball at his chest. Hard.

"Whoa! Down, girl. I was just kidding."

The game became their focus—she made the next layup

shot easily. He caught it, cross dribbled, then jumped high and sunk a slam dunk. They guarded one another aggressively but were careful to avoid fouls—each of them acutely aware of the other's physical space. For the next few minutes they seemed equally matched until he tried an inside shot that rebounded off the backboard without going in. Maybe, she thought, swiping the ball and making the basket, he's even more distracted than I am.

"Game!" she yelled joyously, catching her own rebound.

"You beat me," he said, giving her her props.

"Not by much," she rejoined. "Were you the star forward on your school team before coming here?" Knowing damn well he wasn't.

He shook his head. "I'm not much for team play."

"Yet if you played for Brighurst, it might make you feel more part of things."

"Who said I wanted to be part of things? I'm just logging time until—"

"What? College?" she asked, surprised at how badly she wanted to know everything she could.

He sucked in a long breath. "I'm not into planning." He strode around her. "And how about you, Ms. Courtney Bryant? How come I don't see you in a Brighurst girls' basketball uniform? Or is it not up to your sartorial standards?" His sarcasm cut.

"Yeah, that's the reason," she finally said, "I don't like the uniforms."

He grimaced. "Hey, I'm sorry. That was stupid."

"And unfair," she added. "You barely know me. You're treating me like some stereotype."

He shrugged, and began dribbling the ball in a circle around her. "Just like everyone here treats me, like some low-life migrant worker who accidentally backed into Brighurst."

Courtney colored, remembering Shelby's comment when Jake turned up at her party. She ducked, and grabbed the ball away from him. "So maybe some people are quick to categorize, to point fingers. It doesn't mean we're all like that—"

Jake swiped the ball away from her. Suddenly, he was right in front of her. Bordering her personal space.

"—It doesn't mean *we* have to be like them," she finished her thought.

They were closer now, nearly touching. He leaned in and she tilted her face up to meet his.

The long shiny black limo bearing the Delmonico's logo appeared at the back gate.

Jake cut his eyes toward it; his jaw tightened. "Your carriage has arrived, princess. You oughta go."

Courtney frowned. Who knew a Rolls limo could be a buzz kill? She rallied with a carefree shrug and inviting smile. "We're both going back to the Del. You should come with."

He smirked. "And experience how the other half rides? I'll pass." He grabbed the ball roughly, and began dribbling it toward the basket. He'd turned his back on her, so his face registered surprise as she came from the side and took control of the ball.

"It's just a car. It gets you from point A to point B. Don't be so stubborn."

For a microsecond, Jake seemed about to growl at her. Thinking better of it, he replied, "Well, if all cars are created equal, why don't you come in mine? Like you said, we're going the same way."

His words were meant to be a challenge. But his heart wasn't in it. At that moment Courtney learned something about Jake Martinez that nothing in his file could have told her. He'd been beaten down, he was sad . . . and he was as confused as she was.

"So what d'ya say," he pushed, "send your luxury limo packin' and come in my car? It's got a name, too. We call it the Crapmobile."

Courtney's heart raced. Out of the blue a song lyric came to her. Her dad's old Springsteen CD, something about, " . . . *if you're ready to take that long walk, from your front porch to my front seat, the door's open but the ride ain't free . . .*"

This much Courtney knew: A ride in Jake's car was going to cost her.

Chapter 11

Going All the Way

The Crapmobile was aptly named. Outside: rust patches, mismatched hubcaps, banged-in side panel. Inside: ripped seats, no CD or tape player, busted radio. But that didn't rattle her so much as the fact that she was inches away from Jake's tanned, muscular body.

That, and the fact that they were going the wrong way.

"Do you know how to get back to Delmonico's?" she asked.

"I do," he answered, keeping his amazing eyes on the road ahead.

"So where are we going?"

"Anywhere but there."

Courtney took in a quick breath, and considered. She'd told her Girls she'd probably meet up with them, but hadn't promised. Her date with Liam wasn't until eight-thirty. There wasn't anyplace she had to be for several hours.

They were headed onto Desert Inn Road, a major boulevard, heading east, away from the sun. If they took it far
enough, they'd be deep in the desert. But Courtney had a better idea.

"I know a place by Lake Mead, a little café," she piped up.
"It's on the Northshore Drive."

"Let's do it," he agreed.

She was less nervous than she should have been.

What did she really know about this stranger at the wheel?
Other than he'd been ripped from his home turf just before his
senior year—and was furious about it? That he hated every
second at Brighurst, and wasn't too psyched at playing waiter
at Delmonico's? She'd intuited his rage the first day she'd seen
him, stepping out of the elevator, right into her party, where
the night ended with punches being thrown.

No way should she allow herself to be alone with him,
armed with only her wits and a cell phone. Which might not
even work if they went farther than Lake Mead.

Okay, she'd take a chance just this once, get the curiosity
out of her system. And be done with it.

They drove for another twenty-five minutes in silence.
Partly because the clanging of the car's broken muffler made
conversation difficult, and partly because the scenery spoke
volumes. The dramatic landscape of nature's desert—as op-
posed to Las Vegas's man-made kind—spread out before them.
When they turned up the Northshore Drive, Lake Mead appeared, a sparkling, glistening blue, surrounded by the grays,
blacks, reds, and browns of the surrounding boulders, rock
formations, and mountains. She tried to gauge his reaction to
the tranquil beauty, but Jake's face revealed nothing.

"The place is at the next turn-in," Courtney shouted over the muffler's din.

It looked like any random "scenic view" picnic area, but the road continued, curving and twisting for another mile or so until they came to a low, flat stucco building. A painted wooden sign over the door gave its name: THE STAR THROWER CAFÉ.

Jake shot her a glance. "Don't tell me this is your hangout. Unless they're dealing something else in the backroom, I can't picture *you* coming here."

Courtney chuckled. "Shows what you know. I used to come here all the time. With my dad."

Jake parked the car, and she led him through the simple, shadowy café to a patio of round tables with umbrellas in back. Below them, down at the far bottom of a steep slope, was the lake in all its shimmering beauty.

This time, Jake couldn't hide the awe in his eyes, or the sharp intake of breath. It was an amazing sight.

They sat beside one another on a bench at a wooden picnic table. A waitress came with menus and they ordered a home-made margherita pizza to share and a pitcher of lemonade.

"So"—Jake waved his muscled arm at the scenery—"is this part of the 'other side of Vegas' sightseeing tour?"

"Is that a bad thing?" Courtney inquired.

He allowed, "Well, it's better than Brighurst. But I won't be getting out here much. I'm an indentured slave to the hotel, on the most nauseating, crass-tastic strip of land in the world."

She let the indentured servant remark pass. "The Strip *is* sort of overwhelming, a kind of Disneyland for adults. But doesn't L.A. have that same glitzy unreality . . . I mean, with Hollywood and all?"

He stared at her, his dark eyes accusing. "How do you know where I'm from?"

I stole your file from the dean's office.

My dad must have mentioned it.

I spent the last few hours in the library devouring your file.

Our chief of staff, Bill Martin, told me.

I'm obsessed with you.

I make it my business to know everything about our staff.

Tell the truth, tell a lie. A roulette wheel spun in her head. She didn't know where the little ball would land. She studied him carefully. The eyes, said the cliché, may be windows to the soul, but in Jake's case? Not so much. He wasn't wearing hip designer sunglasses, but he might as well have had blackout shades pulled down over them. They were inscrutable, revealing nothing. Only that the glinting flashes of anger clashed with his soft, clean-shaven cheeks, his full lips. And that his defined cheekbones and nose that'd seen its share of breaks didn't go with that kick-ass pair of dimples. The rough, hardened hands and the obvious intellect? Another disconnect.

Jake was a paradox, a conundrum.

Shaking, Courtney ducked into her bag and pulled out the manila folder marked MARTINEZ, JACOB.

His wariness ramped to anger. "You . . . have my file? What gives you the freakin' right? Or is there nothing off-limits to you in this town?" He shot up, ready to leave, but she grabbed his elbow. "Please, don't, Jake. I can explain. I want to—"

She could see the wheels spinning in his head as he sized her up. Stomp away in a righteous huff? Allow her to talk to him? Kill her, or trust her?

Cautiously, he slung one leg back over the bench, unsure.

"So you know I'm from East L.A. It's where the other half lives, the working class, if you're lucky. It's where real human beings are born, bred, and die. And I wish I'd never left."

"Why did you?" she asked, unblinkingly.

His jaw clenched, his eyes scanned the lake. The silence was broken only when the waitress appeared with the pitcher of lemonade, pouring glasses over ice for both of them.

Finally, Jake said, "My moms passed last July. Cancer. But I guess you already knew that."

Courtney said gently, "It didn't say when she died. I'm sorry . . . for your loss."

His eyes glistened lethally. "Yeah, thanks."

"What was she like?" Courtney asked.

"Cool lady. Proud, smart, funny as hell. But she never understood that I was good, I was happy where I was. She kept pushing the education thing, saying I needed to get out, move up. College, that'd give me choices in life. While she was in the hospital at the end, she made me promise . . ."

His voice caught; quickly, he looked away.

Courtney put her hand on his arm, but he brushed it off.

"I told her I'd graduate high school and go to college. Coming here was the only way I could keep that promise. Is that good enough for you, or do you require the rest of the sordid details?"

The anger had returned, mitigating the pain etched across his face. And Courtney fought a lump in her throat. "You loved her, you miss her. I'm really sorry," she whispered.

He nodded, staring at the horizon.

Courtney felt the hot shame of her own tears—tears!—gliding down her face. She didn't even know this boy, why was she internalizing his pain?

Before she could grab for a napkin, Jake turned around. He eyed her quizzically. "So where's your mom? Been here long enough to know she doesn't live at the Del."

Courtney dabbed at her eyes. "You're right, she doesn't."

"Dead?" Jake ventured.

"I wouldn't know," Courtney responded, as casually as she could manage. "She split when I was a kid, haven't heard from, or about, her since."

Nor had she cried over her mom. Ever.

"That's tough, I guess," Jake said, "being abandoned like that. Not even all the money or privilege in the world makes up for that. You still feel like you weren't good enough or something, not good enough for her to have stayed."

"Who died and made you Confucius?" Courtney was suddenly irked, and ready to bolt.

"Whoa, overreacting much, princess?"

Abandoned. She hadn't been abandoned. OK, so her mom, Delia Bryant, hadn't died, she'd chosen to leave. Whatever. Maybe her father had felt deserted at the time. Courtney, only two years old, was collateral damage. They'd both healed very well, thank you! She and her dad had done amazingly well. Maternal nurturing was overrated.

Though not, she realized, for Jake. Alone through no fault of his own, he felt abandoned, and worse, banished, to some strange land where he didn't, would never, belong. Let alone feel at home.

So what about his bio-dad? Was he but a wealthy sperm-donor who'd walked away from the responsibility of an unwanted child? And had the father only now reappeared because Jake's mom had died—only to do what was convenient for himself, no matter what impact it had on his son?

Jake had told her as much as he would—for today, at least. As for the rest, who his dad really was, and why Jake was going to the most expensive private school in Las Vegas, yet toiling as a waiter?

That mystery would unravel in time.

The lake, serene, glittering now in the late day sun, mesmerized them. And that was a good thing.

Her cell phone rang, breaking the mood. She ignored it.

Which seemed to amuse Jake. "Bet that was one of your friends wondering where you are. Gonna tell 'em where you really are?"

"Why wouldn't I?" she challenged.

"Because," he countered, "they might not approve of who you're with."

"Stereotyping much? They're not like the other girls at Brighurst. Taryn doesn't care what anybody thinks of her and Reign is always up for something daring. Leesa might be—"

"Reign del Castille, daring?" he interrupted skeptically. "Give me a break. She's just a spoiled brat desperate for attention. What could be more pathetic?"

"You don't even know her!" Courtney objected, realizing Jake wasn't so removed from Brighurst that he hadn't heard the shame-on-Reign scuttlebutt.

He laughed derisively. "Reign is much too impressed with herself to bother with someone like me. I know as much about her as I need to know."

"You should give her a chance," Courtney insisted.

"I don't think so."

The pizza arrived and they cut into it. The basil on top of the slabs of fresh-made mozzarella cheese gave the thin-crust pizza a unique flavor. He commented. "Never had designer pizza like this at home, or limos, or any of the trappings you probably couldn't live without. But I had friends there, homies who had my back. The people on my block were like a family. When my mom was in the hospital, someone invited me to eat over every night: they took care of me, would've kept taking care of me. I never wanted to leave them, but . . ." He trailed off, focused on the horizon.

"It's hard, I get it—" Without thinking, Courtney put her hand on his arm. She'd meant to comfort him, to show empathy . . . but she felt the electricity. His skin was hot. And not just from the desert sun.

Jake whipped around so quickly, he toppled the bench. Courtney would have fallen backwards. Only he caught her in his strong arms. And she caught him right back. Neither let go.

There was nothing tentative or exploring about their kiss. It was so intense, it felt like a battle. His mouth on hers, hers pressing harder on his. His tongue . . . everywhere, her teeth everywhere. They couldn't pull away, not even to gasp for air.

Desire.

Pure and simple, and hard and painful.

Finally, they loosened their embrace. She had no idea what to do next. He gently drew her to him again, holding her close with the flat of his hand against her upper back. It was such a tender gesture after the intensity of that kiss. A strange, wonderful sensation arose inside her, as though this loving touch had unexpectedly freed something deep inside that had been locked in a cage.

Then Courtney's cell phone rang. Again.

"Maybe you'd best answer it," Jake whispered.

Checking the caller ID, she saw it was Reign. And that it was 7 P.M.! "Oh, no, I forgot to call Reign! I was going to . . . we were supposed to meet, I was going to tell her to go on without me—only . . . shit!"

"They might be worried about you," he speculated, without irony. "How late are you?"

"About two hours," she admitted.

"Best call her back then," he said pointing out the obvious.

Nodding, she speed-dialed her friend. "It's me. Look, I got delayed. You guys eat without me. I'll explain later. Bye."

"Will you?" he asked.

"What?"

"Explain later?"

She drew in a long, slow breath. "I don't know," she admitted.

"Will you tell them you were slumming . . . making out with the Chicano help?" he cracked, not unkindly.

Slowly, she shook her head. "No. We don't lie to each other, me and my Girls."

He studied her, considering her words. "Okay. Fair enough. I believe you." He spoke as if he were talking to himself more than to her. "Besides, I can't say what the truth is—can you? What we're really doing here. Your guess is as good as mine, princess."

* * *

Jake dropped her off at the main entrance to the Delmonico, and drove around back to the staff quarters. Traffic had slowed them, and it was late, really late. Fifteen-minutes-before-Liam-was-due late. She rushed into the lobby, practically colliding with Leesa and Reign. "Hi, you guys," she greeted them, hoping she didn't sound as guilty as she felt.

"What happened to you?" Reign demanded. "I had left two messages."

Leesa observed, "Your hair is a wreck, your makeup is smudged—and not stylishly. And you're in . . . sneakers? Did you have gym detention? I'm confused."

"Great to see you, too," Courtney volleyed back, trying to sound cute.

"Well, where were you?!" Reign ranted. "Taryn didn't show either. So—what? you think one spa visit, and everything's fine? Well, it isn't!"

"You don't have to jump all over her," Leesa scolded Reign. "She's just late. Cut her some slack."

Courtney apologized. "I lost track of the time. I'm sorry."

"You're sorry, yeah, right," Reign said sulkily. "You know this whole thing with Brad has me freaked. You're supposed to be there for me. Twenty-four seven. I just know he's getting it on with someone else."

Leesa put her arm around Reign. "No, you do not know that."

Yeah, he probably is, thought Courtney, but she wouldn't hurt Reign by saying it.

"What were you doing all this time, anyway?" Reign went at Courtney again.

"I played a little pickup game of basketball," she replied, still trying to avoid a full-on lie.

"Basketball?" Reign cried incredulously.

"It's good exercise. Why not?" she countered.

"With who?" Reign pressed.

"A bunch of kids," Courtney said evasively.

"Incoming, ladies—check it out, three o'clock," Leesa alerted them.

The revolving door gave a quarter turn—and out popped Courtney's erstwhile curly-haired beau. A million mixed-up emotions blasted through her at the sight of her handsome, athletic Liam. Guilt being at the top of the list. He'd come to pick her up; she was far, far from ready. She'd lost track of time because she'd been making out with . . . someone else.

"Hey!" he greeted them with a wave of his hand. The friendly, trusting expression on his face did nothing to assuage her guilt.

"Gotta go," she said, backing away from Reign and Leesa, toward Liam. What was she going to tell *him* now?

"Hey, babe, running late?" he said, kissing her lightly. He was so trusting. Shit.

"I am," she confessed, "I'm really sorry. Come on upstairs with me and I'll be ready in a sec." She waved to Leesa and Reign as she hurried toward the private elevator. Reign eyed her suspiciously. That girl needed lots more help than a simple spa intervention, Courtney thought. Nothing less than banishing Brad from her life was going to really help.

They went to the penthouse, directly to Courtney's bedroom, where she grabbed the remote and switched on ESPN for Liam. "I'll just shower and be right out," she told him.

Courtney peeled her top off as she entered her bathroom, lightly kicking the door shut behind her. She pressed the button for steam and stepped into the wide glass stall, letting the hot mist swirl around her.

It was a relief to finally be alone where she could unwind—

and rewind. Without meaning to, she replayed the kiss—over and over. It was so much better than her dream had been, more intense, more of a connection than she'd ever made with anyone before.

Running her fingers down her body, she thought of Jake and how his every taut muscle had seemed to ache for her. Feeling sultry, she leaned against the tile wall and let the steam work its way along her skin like his hot caressing hand. Her eyes slid shut. "Jake," she whispered.

Her eyes shot open; instantly she stopped fantasizing. This was not good, on so many levels.

Shutting off the steam, she turned on the shower and began furiously lathering her hair as she forced herself to think about the gorgeous "match" just a few feet away on the other side of the bathroom wall. She and Liam had been together for over six months. They'd hooked up, sure—they just hadn't done *everything*. Courtney had always stopped short, unsure why exactly. She'd know when the time was right for her and Liam. Wouldn't she? It would be organic, it would just happen when it was meant to.

Or maybe, she thought, struggling to push aside images of Jake, of her head resting on his shoulder, of feeling safe, of feeling so passionate that she wanted to jump out of her own skin . . . maybe you *decided* when the moment was right. Maybe you made the connection by getting proactive with the right person.

Liam. Where would she ever find a sweeter guy? In all the months they'd been together he hadn't ever pressed himself on her; hadn't insisted that they do any more than she was willing to do. And here she was in a lather over a guy she hardly knew, when Liam—who was the real deal, who fit perfectly into her world—was right there waiting for his chance to be with her.

Courtney turned off the shower and patted herself dry. She stepped into the bedroom—wearing only the towel.

"Almost ready?" Liam asked, glued to the soccer game on the plasma set.

"Maybe we should stay in tonight," she suggested coyly.

"Sure," he agreed, turning casually toward her. "If you want we could order . . ." He went slack-jawed at the sight of her, standing there in only a towel.

She let it drop to her feet.

In seconds they were on each other, kissing frantically. "God, you're sexy," he whispered huskily as they fell together onto her bed.

She pulled his shirt over his head and then went for the zipper of his jeans. "Got a condom?" she asked.

He stopped and looked searchingly into her eyes. Her question had taken him by surprise.

"Do you?" she repeated.

He nodded, reaching for the wallet in his back pocket.

Liam's expression was a mixture of delight and concern. "Are you sure?" Courtney nodded and worked her hand down into his jeans. Liam lifted himself on top of her.

She closed her eyes while he ran his eager hands along her body. Her eyes remained closed as he positioned himself between her legs. She began to float away on the sweet, sweet sensation.

Soon she was lost in the motion as they rocked together. She fell into a half dream; she was on a basketball court. Jake was on top of her right there, out in the open. She was writhing beneath him, moaning with pleasure. She wanted to look into his dark chocolate eyes, to see his soul, to witness him wanting, needing, having her.

Only when she looked up, the sea foam blue-green of Liam's eyes stared down at her.

Courtney's hand flew to her mouth. "Oh, my God!"

She was in the middle of a threesome. Jake in her head, Liam on her body. And she had no control whatsoever.

Abruptly, she rolled away from him. "I can't!" she sputtered, "I—I'm so sorry."

"Babe, what's the matter?" he asked, upset and frustrated.

"I thought I was ready, but I'm not," she blurted out. She buried her face in her hands, more confused than she'd ever been in her life.

Chapter 12

Reign, Reign, Falling Down

Leesa, the last friend standing, as far as Reign was concerned, was doing her best to be supportive, to help Reign deal with her Brad trauma. This was their second time power-shopping, since the first one, a week ago, hadn't worked.

The girls trolled every store at the Delmonico, from Betsey Johnson to Rocawear, from FCUK to bebe, from Haute Diggity Dog to Three Blind Dice to Sex Kitten.

Reign felt nothing. Nada. Zilch. No matter what hot accessory or latest must-have Leesa showed her, Reign could not get psyched. They'd been at it for hours. Glitterati was the last stop on the shopping express.

"I can't believe there's nothing in the entire galleria you want," Leesa wailed, " 'cause you know I'd snag anything for you, and retail therapy has proven emotional benefits. I don't know why you're being so resistant."

Reign's shoulders sagged. "Everything here is material—by definition, disposable." Like she was to Brad.

Deflated, Leesa gently probed, "So how can I help? We all want to."

All of them? So where were Courtney and Taryn?

Sure, Courtney got props for the spa intervention. From behind the stiff curtain of her mud mask Reign had told her friends about Brad's rejection. The Girls had been furious, disbelieving, but rational. Unloading onto Court, Taryn, and Leesa had made her feel better, a huge improvement over dealing with that Botoxed shrinky-dink her parents had so much faith in.

But Reign had not disclosed all. No one knew Brad had asked to borrow money. That was too shameful to confess. Worse, that she'd given it to him.

Leesa squeezed her shoulder. "We've got some amazing totes. I think you'll flip over the Dior detective bag—it's got all these secret pockets, inspired by mystery movies. And it comes in red, black, or cream. Perfect for you!"

Tote *this,* Reign wanted to say.

Courtney, Taryn, Leesa. Didn't any of them realize how serious this was? What if one of their boyfriends had a homegirl hookup? Reign was sure, very sure, that he was making it with someone.

Leesa held up three Dior detective satchels, large, medium, and small, in red, black, and cream. "Nearly impossible to get," Leesa said. "Uma's all about these; so is Penelope Cruz."

Reign barely heard her. Brad did not want to kiss her, touch her, hook up with her. He'd asked for a handout. She'd acquiesced . . . why? Because it was the only way left to connect with him right now. Was it enough to bring him back to her, when his latest money emergency was over? Would he remember she was the one who saved his ass? And if he did, would he be into her, would he want her, the way he used to? Or would he just be . . . grateful?

That'd be the worst.

"Here's the one I had to give to Shelby," Leesa was saying, now displaying a small studded flap-pocket Gucci purse with a bamboo handle, "in ostrich, would you believe?"

"Had to?" Finally, Leesa caught Reign's attention. "Why? What's that snarky string bean got on you?"

Leesa blushed. "Nothing really. She was just . . . uh . . . she said she'd share some advance gossip in exchange for cutting the line to snag that bag. She paid for it, totally. I just bumped her up."

And what gossip was worth that? Reign would have asked, but what was the point? Leesa sucked at lying. She couldn't tell a falsehood from a Juicy hood.

Unlike Reign, who'd been born with an internal lie-detector. The needle of which had gone off the chart when Courtney had blown into the hotel last week, late, sweaty, and oozing guilt from every perfect pore. Playing basketball? With some kids? Right, like Courtney had ever done that in her entire life! Not only a lie, but a lame one.

If there was any bouncing or dribbling during Courtney's afternoon away from her friends, there was a guy involved.

"Ouch! That hurts!"

Leesa clutched her arm so tightly, Reign was sure there'd be a red mark. "Look who it is!" Leesa shrieked, as if Elvis in fact *was* in the building.

Only it was no chubby, sideburned icon strutting down the hallway of the Delmonico. It was IZOD preppy boy himself, Bradley Simmons, shirt untucked, hair porcupining in all directions, coming from the main casino in the lobby.

Reign's heart did a flip-flop. And she couldn't stop the smile from spreading across her face. Just the sight of him, so sure, so confident, yet so vulnerable underneath it all—something only she knew—tripped her inner mush-o-meter.

The lobby and shopping arcade were in full happy-go-hubbub mode, packed with guests. Brad didn't see them.

"Brad!" Leesa called out.

Reign made for him, but his pace picked up—intentionally? Nah, he hadn't even heard them. Brad had a lot on his mind.

Only where was he running? From gambling debts, or . . . she realized he might've been coming from the elevator . . . from someone's room? Stopping in her tracks, she studied him before he reached the revolving doors and headed out. Reign read his body language.

That's when her heart sank. His shoulders were taut, his head down. He looked guilty.

Math was not her best subject. But it didn't take the genius that Russell Crowe played in *A Beautiful Mind* to put two and screw together.

Courtney? Rushing in late last week and lookin' guilty.

Brad? Ducking out of the hotel Courtney lived in. Lookin' guilty.

The "bimbo" Brad was doing, right under her nose, here in Vegas? The reason he no longer wanted Reign? Whaddya' know, Liam *and* Brad.

Courtney Bryant was double-dipping.

* * *

Betrayal.

The hurt felt like a steel-heeled stiletto puncturing her heart. The rage felt like she could rip the world apart with her teeth. There wasn't anything she didn't want to smash, but the thing she most wanted to pulverize was Courtney Bryant's heart-shaped face.

All these years, from being pinky-swearing bff's, to bffl's, to the Glossy Posse, to now just "the Girls"—had that all been rendered meaningless the minute Courtney had decided to steal Reign's boyfriend? Or had Courtney never been sincere? Had she, like all the others, pretended to be Reign's close personal friend because she was Hollywood royalty, which trumped Courtney's own Vegas sovereignty?

Did Courtney secretly harbor red-carpet ambitions? Did she think Reign could snag her a starring role in some movie? Or maybe it'd always been about name-check currency: "I spent the weekend with my Girl, Reign del Castille. Yeah, in fact, she is the daughter of Lola Marquez and Stefan del Castille. Yep, that one, the Oscar winner."

Betrayal.

It hurt like hell. It burned her, it enraged her. And it made her more paranoid than ever.

Leaving Leesa at the galleria, Reign did something she never thought she'd stoop to. Like a scene from one of her mom's ridiculous spy movies, she followed Brad. Ducking out of the hotel, she positioned herself amid a group of tourists so he wouldn't spot her.

She watched him give the valet his ticket.

A few minutes later, she jumped into a cab, and instructed the driver to "follow that Porsche."

If Brad was coming off a quick booty call with Courtney, he'd likely head straight back to the frat house. But if she'd been wrong about Courtney, if Brad had someone else—possibly he was headed there now. Somewhere, deep inside, she knew her hurt and confusion were leading down an irrational path. But she went there anyway.

From the backseat of a filthy, smelly Vegas cab—ugh, did people actually ride in these?—she kept her eyes peeled on the driver of the Porsche. His cell phone was pressed to his ear. Was he telling some girl he was on his way? Or purring to someone else about the scorching visit they'd just shared? She checked the readout on her own phone. He wasn't calling her.

She punched in Courtney's number. And got voice mail. Court was on the phone with someone else, not picking up when she beeped in.

Brad crossed into the turn lane, signaling that he was making a right on Tropicana Avenue. The frat house was a block south, on East Flamingo.

* * *

It was after 10 P.M. when Reign got home. She hadn't realized how much a stinky taxi could charge, when you took it from the hotel to a UNLV frat house, then all the way across town to her family's heavily guarded Summerlin estate. She was grateful for her Mini Cooper, and the family limo.

She was surprised to find her mother, tiny inside her La Perla robe, her personal assistant, Daryn, plus Ginger,

Starshine, and Haven, all on the sectional in the great room, watching a *CSI* rerun on the big-screen plasma TV.

"Oh, Lola, you were so fabulous in that scene!" Daryn gushed. Ginger wryly noted, "You should have gotten a guest star Emmy; you were robbed."

Lola, soaking up the adoration of her at-home fan club, didn't notice Reign traipsing through the room. By the time she looked up at her downtrodden daughter, Ginger had already offered to make Reign a snack, Daryn had noted there was room on the couch if she wanted to join them, and Star had asked if she could borrow Reign's D&G bag for tomorrow.

Reign turned down the offers and flung the bag in Starshine's direction. Like she cared.

Upstairs, she locked the door to her suite, and paced. Her tears ramped up into wracking sobs, as she viciously shredded her formerly favorite snapshots—any with Courtney or Brad in them—kicked the divan, and set a match to the plush panda slippers Courtney had given her.

The smoke set off the fire alarm. Which eventually, after her dad's butler broke in, doused the flames, and flung open the windows, brought Lola to the door. Without preamble, her mother said, "What's going on, Reign? If you're trying to burn the house down, you might want to start with the kitchen."

Reign backed away from Lola, petite, dazzlingly dark-haired, luminous even without makeup. "It was an accident, it won't happen again."

Lola surveyed the trashed bedroom. "Sweetheart, you know you can confide in me."

Because you've always been so understanding? So intuitive? As if you have any clue what I'm feeling right now? Reign didn't articulate that. She shook her head no, and perched on her bed.

She'd assumed Lola, relieved, would swish grandly out of the room. But her mother didn't move. Nor speak. Lola regarded Reign as carefully as she ever had, then finally said, "Okay then. If you change your mind, call me on my cell phone. I'll be in my sauna."

"Of course you will." Reign's head was lowered, as she took off her shoes. She didn't care if her mom heard her or not.

Reign finally cried herself to sleep.

When she awoke the next morning, she was reenergized. That is, freshly enraged and newly wounded.

She snapped at the family cook at breakfast, kicked Haven's sneakers across the living room, and growled at Starshine in the limo on the way to school. Star, her middle sister, was the spitting image of Lola, from her petite bone structure to her long, silky, shimmering black hair, which she wore down to her waist. Haven, also an exquisite beauty, had somehow inherited the best of Stefan, his piercing bittersweet chocolate eyes, his wide angular cheekbones, his caramel skin, plus her mother's delicate nose and full lips.

In her most self-pitying moods, Reign felt like the "first pass," the "out-of-town" tryout—a screenplay or production that ought to have been scrapped in favor of the ones they got right later on.

* * *

In the mornings during her sophomore year, when he was still a student at Brighurst, Brad used to come to her locker. A little saliva swapping and a well-placed squeeze of her "sweet cheeks" before homeroom, he'd joke, could get him through the most boring day. He'd actually promised her "phone squeezes" when they talked about his going to UNLV while she was still at Brighurst. As she fumbled with her locker combination, her mind wandered. Just how long had Courtney and Brad been at it?

Sweet cheeks. When had he last called her that?

At the party! Yes, it had to have been! No wonder he'd been so rude to her that night. He'd been showing off for Courtney, proving he was over Reign. Despite her display of solidarity that night, secretly Courtney must have eaten up that little display. It burned Reign to think of it.

Fueled by rage, blinded by the injustice of it all, she powered down the hall to her first-period class. Wheeling around the corner, she barreled right into a stationary object, of the human variety. Oh, how she wished it could've been Brad—or better, Courtney.

But when she looked up, she saw only the shocked face of some random student, totally stealthed by the head-on with Reign.

"Whoa!" he exclaimed, "Hit the brakes, will ya?"

Reign didn't apologize. Why should she? "Just move, okay? You're in the way."

"What is it with you people? You think you're such hot shots that it's okay to bash into anyone in your path?" He laced into her accusingly.

Who the hell was he? Reign regarded him angrily. He was—! Oh, man, the creep from the party, that insolent waiter. The one who punched Liam. Jake, wasn't it? The one they'd been trying to unravel the mystery about, like how he got into Brighurst, and who was paying the bill. That's who was giving her lip?

She snarled at him, "You're not worth the time to argue with. Out of my way, loser!"

His face morphed into a mask of disgust. "I don't think *you* want to be calling me a loser," he barked back at her menacingly.

Who did he think he was threatening? And the arrogant, dangerous look on his face! "I'll call you whatever I want," she countered fiercely. And then she shouted words she hadn't since first grade: "Do you know who my parents are?"

Only he didn't react like an awestruck grade school student. Quietly, he said, "I do. The question really is, Do you?"

Just then, Courtney rounded the corner and stopped short. "What's the matter?" she asked. "What's going on?"

The sight of Courtney acted like a chemical accelerator, fueling and increasing Reign's seething rage. She felt an overwhelming impulse to punch Courtney.

But she couldn't.

There was a lump in her throat suddenly, tears were threatening. She swallowed them back. This was Courtney's turf, and no one—not even her—whaled on the power princess. Even if Courtney had only been feigning friendship, and turned out to be a backstabbing, boyfriend-robbing bitch. Reign didn't have the courage to confront her.

Courtney was a damn good actress, Reign would give her that. Pretending she couldn't imagine what had Reign so riled up, Courtney's turquoise eyes were as open and sincere as a newborn pup's.

But this abusive waiter was annoying the hell out of her.

Jake made a move to walk away, turning his back on her.

It was all the provocation Reign needed. Her face clenched like a fist, she flew forward, and without thinking, slapped him hard across the face.

Stunned, Jake stood there a half second, then came toward her, his palm open and ready to strike. He was inches from her face when he stopped abruptly.

Courtney's hand was wrapped around his wrist. "Stop it! Stop! What are you doing?" she screamed. Freaked out, she ran to Reign's side, but Reign brusquely shouldered her out of the way, and rushed off down the hall.

* * *

She returned home that afternoon to the sound of shouting. Her mother was on her cell phone, pacing the living room, screaming at someone. "Can't you get rid of him? Give him money or something," she shrieked.

Noticing Reign, Lola switched to Spanish, something her father and mother had always done when they did not want their English-speaking children eavesdropping. Through the years, Reign had picked up some Spanish. Enough to get the gist of Lola's angry words. *I forgave you. I didn't walk out on you. I told you to do what you have to. I don't want to know the details. I don't want to meet him!*

"*Basta! Nada mas!*" She slammed the phone closed, and threw it at the wall, where it bounced and fell to the hardwood floor in several pieces.

Reign stared at her. She'd had the worst day ever. On the ride home, she'd even considered opening up to Lola—about

Courtney, Brad, and even that sketchy scene in the hallway with waiter-boy. But, what a surprise, Lola was in the midst of her own drama right now.

"Was that Dad you were on the phone with?" Reign asked.

"It was *nobody*," her mother replied, choking on her words. "Nobody at all."

Her mother whirled, seeming to see Reign clearly for the first time. "Did you want to talk to me about something?"

About to say no, Reign heard herself saying, "There is something—but maybe you're too upset right now."

"Go on," Lola urged her, fighting to get back to calm. "Sometimes it's better to have someone to talk to."

Reign perched on the arm of one of the imposing wing chairs in the living room, smoothed her jeans, and screwed up her courage. "Say there was a guy. Going with this girl. For a long time. They were more than just casual hookups. Between them, it was the real thing."

Lola rolled her phenomenal tricolor eyes. "Trouble in paradise?"

"I didn't say it was about me," Reign bristled. And then it all came spilling out. "I'm just saying. Theoretically. Like the girl suspects . . . I mean, knows, that he's got someone else. She even knows who the someone else is. Probably. But she's still into him. And wants him back. Do you know any tricks to get him back? Like if you really, really, you know, kind of loved him?"

"Dump him!" Lola suddenly roared, pointing at her daughter. "Brad. You mean Brad, right? He's a cheating pig—just like your father!"

Chapter 13

Shopping Savant Spies Star Sib with Golf Course Scion

"I can't wait to get my hands on that bag," Shelby trilled excitedly as she followed Leesa into Glitterati. They walked past counters of designer tops, shoes, and jewelry before stopping at the glass counter featuring scarves and handbags.

"Hi, Carol," Leesa said to the petite saleswoman. "You have one of the new Gucci bags for Shelby Alexis?"

Carol checked a list then opened a case and took out the bag, placing it on the counter. As advertised, it was underarm small, accessorized with lots of hardware, and retailed for close to five thousand dollars.

Shelby practically had an orgasm. She plunked down her platinum credit card, and bragged to Carol, "Being friends with Leesa Tenley has its perks."

Carol gave her a tight smile, and Leesa felt a gag reflex coming, without any encouragement. She'd hoped Shelby would take her new bag and leave but the girl seemed in no hurry and began browsing casually through a pile of beaded cashmere shrug jackets.

"They work if you've got on something strapless on a cool evening," Leesa commented for the sake of conversation. "But shrugs are a fad that'll be so over in no time."

Ignoring Leesa, Shelby mused, "I could use one of these." She pulled a hot pink shrug from the pile and hurried to a mirror to try it on.

Not interested in the merchandise—nothing new had come in lately—and especially bored with Shelby, Leesa wandered out in front of the store. Taking out her cell phone, she began a text message to Courtney, just to say hi and complain about being stuck with Shelby, when an elevator door opened and Brad walked out. He was talking animatedly to someone who was still in the elevator so Leesa took a step back into the store doorway, interested to see who he was with without being spotted by him.

Starshine del Castille came out of the elevator next and Leesa's suspicious expression relaxed. He was with Reign's sister. She was about to step forward and say hi when they ducked into Blingtones, the high-end jewelry store. Leesa tried to make the connection between Brad and Starshine. Then it hit her! *Reign's birthday!* It was coming up in a few weeks.

Brad was probably in search of a gift for Reign. A gift that not only said "Happy Birthday," but also whispered, "My bad. I'm sorry." And, "I'm ready for some lovin'."

'Cause nothing, in Leesa's experience, gave a girl more incentive to give it up than bling.

To show real sincerity, Brad had brought the sister with

him. Who'd know Reign's taste better than Starshine? Leesa felt secure that she'd been right all along. Whatever'd been going down between Brad and Reign would be patched up by Reign's birthday.

Leesa went back to touch base with Shelby and found the girl sitting on a cushioned bench among boxes of shoes. Carol, the saleswoman, grimaced. Shelby rarely thought of anyone whose job it was to wait on her as human, even, let alone worthy of consideration. "Let me see this pair of slings in turquoise with pink beads. And while you're at it, let me see it in an eight, eight and a half, and a nine. Bring the black with green beads in those sizes, too."

Carol caught Leesa's eye for a millisecond with a look that said, *What a pain in the ass!*

Shelby noticed Leesa and looked up with a smile. "My feet swell at certain times of the month and I'm never sure what size I should buy."

"Maybe you should get one in each size," Leesa suggested. As long as Shelby was going to monopolize Carol's time, she might as well get a substantial commission check out of it. "Take your time."

When Carol returned, tottering, buried under a stack of shoe boxes, Leesa wandered back to the front doorway in time to see Brad and Starshine leave the jewelry boutique. Starshine clutched one of the store's signature puff pink paper shopping bags. Leesa was tempted to rush out and ask what they'd bought for Reign, but the elevator door opened and they disappeared into it.

Checking over her shoulder, she saw that Shelby was lost in a reverie of shoe deliberation—holding the turquoise slingback to the light with one hand and inspecting the black pair, which she clutched in the other. An exasperated-looking Carol stood nearby and looked near explosion when Shelby put down the black pair and pointed to a purple-strapped, beaded sandle on a table. Leesa laughed at the sight, despite her sympathy for Carol. This was going to take a while.

Intrigued to know what Brad and Starshine had purchased for Reign, she scurried across the hall into Blingtones. "Hey, Melissa," she greeted the salesclerk behind the wide glass case that sparkled with gold, silver, and gemstones of many colors. Melissa, one of Leesa's least favorite of her father's employees, lived for star sightings and believed that if she read it in *Us, In Touch,* or the *Enquirer,* it must be true.

"You'll never guess who was just in here," Melissa squealed, "Stefan del Castille's daughter! The gorgeous one, with the long black hair like Lola Marquez."

"Give me news, not history." Leesa shot her down. "Her sister's a friend of mine and I wanted to know—"

"Oh, of course," Melissa said, "you're tight with the dumpy oldest one—"

Leesa cut her off. She wasn't having anyone diss her Girl. "Reign has more style in her little pinky than half these string-cheese Hollywood beauties could ever dream of."

Melissa arched her eyebrows, but knew better than to refute her boss's daughter. "Anyway, if it's a news flash you want, how 'bout this? Stefan del Castille and Lola Marquez are going through, as they say, a rough patch. The D word has been dropped."

"Enough!" Leesa was annoyed now. "Stop spreading dirt.

I saw Brad Simmons come in with Starshine. I'm guessing they picked out a birthday gift for Reign. What'd they buy?"

Melissa tapped on the case indicating a necklace. The pendant at the end of the gold chain was a gold star with a diamond in the center.

"That's really classy," Leesa said, relieved, though she herself would've picked a lariat style.

Melissa leaned across the case and her voice took on a low, conspiratorial tone. "Wait until you hear what happened when they went to pay."

"What?" Leesa asked, instinctively lowering her own voice to match Melissa's intriguingly mysterious tone.

"At first that Brad did this whole number about not having his checkbook, and his credit cards being momentarily maxed out. I got the idea that he wanted the sister, Starshine, to put the necklace on her father's tab."

"No!" Leesa gasped. "Was it real expensive?"

Melissa unlocked the case. Reaching in, she turned over the small white price tag that had been discreetly tucked under the pendant. "O-kay," Leesa said, impressed. "That answers my question. Did Star have her dad pay for it?"

Relocking the case, Melissa shook her head. Her eyes danced with enjoyment at the high level of dish she was clearly about to deliver. "She was going to—but get this—when I looked up the del Castilles' account I discovered that her father, Stefan himself, recently made some changes about who was allowed to use it, *and* up to how much money said users could spend."

Leesa was confused. "What are you talking about?"

"Well, I know you think it's all dirty gossip, but maybe in preparation for the divorce, Stefan put serious limits on how much Reign, Star, and Haven may charge now."

"Why would he do that? His latest movie was a huge hit, and he's not in any money trouble I know of," Leesa wondered aloud.

"Well, maybe he had to curb their shopping enthusiasm, because he just added someone to the list who's also allowed to use his charge," Melissa revealed.

Leesa scrunched her forehead. Who would Stefan add?

"Look for yourself," Melissa insisted, leading Leesa over to the computer screen. She quickly typed in his name and Stefan del Castille's account appeared. "The only ones permitted to sign for anything on his account are his wife and some guy," she revealed, "a Mr. Martinez. Who's he?"

"Martinez?" Leesa pondered. "That sounds so familiar."

"Yeah, here it is, J. P. Martinez," Melissa confirmed.

Leesa searched her memory. Was this Martinez guy the del Castilles' manager, a new accountant? The name itself was common enough.

"Anyway," Melissa went on, eager to continue her story, "I was trying to be helpful, so I pulled up Brad's credit info, and guess what? He was flush after all! Apparently, there was money in his account he didn't realize he had. A little weird, but no harm, no foul, he paid for the necklace himself."

That was a relief. Because if Reign ever found out Brad had bought her a birthday gift and charged it to her father, what was left of her shaky self-esteem would crash and burn. "Thanks for sharing."

She waved to Melissa as she ambled out of the store and

back to Glitterati. Shelby was at the counter with her credit card out and six shoe boxes stacked in front of her. "Where did you disappear to?" she inquired with a pout.

"Shel, what's that new guy Jake's last name?" Leesa asked, too distracted to notice or care if Shelby was put out by her absence.

"Something Tex-Mex like Rodriguez, Hernandez, Martinez . . . ," Shelby replied, intensely disinterested.

"Martinez?"

Shelby nodded as she signed her charge. "Could be. Why?"

Leesa was dumbstruck. Could it be that the same Jake Martinez—the waiter—was authorized to charge jewelry on Stefan del Castille's private account?! No, that was too weird to even contemplate.

Timidly, she ventured, "Hey, Shel, has your mom's gossip column mentioned anything about, you know, friction between Reign's parents? 'Cause I've started to hear false rumors, and just wondering what the source might be."

Shelby laughed. "False rumors? Gossipmaven.com does not deal in falsehoods. Here's a tidbit that hasn't even come out yet. Not only are they headed for Splitsville, the even juicier scuttlebutt is that some hot young thing has come between them. And, get this, the hot young thing is young enough to be in high school, at Brighurst!"

"I don't understand," Leesa admitted.

"Oh, it gets better," Shelby said with a knowing smirk. "You know that item my mother ran about a month ago, about some stranger arriving in town, pretending to be who he's not?"

Of course Leesa remembered it—it was the dumb rumor

Courtney had planted to take the scandal spotlight off Reign.
The rumor she made up about someone at Brighurst pretending to be something he's not. The point had been to get people
talking and whispering about who in their midst wasn't what
he seemed. Gossipmaven had co-opted the rumor—and was
now adding fuel to a faux flame.

"Well," Shelby went on, "it seems that someone in the senior class at Brighurst has come between the del Castilles. Someone very hot and male."

Leesa was aghast. "Reign's mom has a younger
boyfriend?"

Shelby began to get frustrated with Leesa's naïve act. "Did
you tune in late or something? We invented the concept of
Cougars in Las Vegas."

"Cougars?" Another stumper.

Shelby was only too happy to educate Leesa. "Cougars.
Older women who hook up with younger men. But—from
what I hear, it isn't necessarily Lola Marquez who's shtupping
the stud."

Leesa colored. No way was she having this convo with
Shelby "skankalicious" Alexis. "Thanks for oversharing,
Shelby. If I were you, I'd tell your mom to check her sources
before she goes spreading dirt around. It's really bad karma."

Shelby shrugged. "You're Reign's close personal friend, I'd
think you'd know all this. Unless Reign is so busy hooking up
with every random thing in pants, that she doesn't know
what's going on in her own household."

"That's enough, Shelby," Leesa said through gritted teeth.
"This conversation is officially over."

"I didn't start it," Shelby reminded her. "Anyway, I've been wondering about you. How're you doing with the . . ." She trailed off, and stuck her finger down her throat, to mimic throwing up.

Just being around Shelby was enough to make Leesa want to hurl.

Chapter 14

Courtney's Keeping Deep Secrets

Courtney's charm bracelets jingled as she applauded the elderly, silver-haired woman scooping coins from the stainless steel bin of the slot machine. "Way to go! That's what Delmonico's likes to see! Big winners!" she cheered.

The woman beamed at her. "My husband and I have spent our anniversary here every year for the last forty years. This place is the best it's ever been, since Dan Bryant took it over. I hear his daughter is his secret weapon."

"She tries," Courtney replied with a smile and a wink. "Go cash in now, and don't give us back too much of your winnings."

Tinkling coins, rattling chips, clinking glasses, and the electronic arpeggios of the slot machines. Whooping winners, mournful losers, soused sinners, sober beginners. The action was fast and furious, the assault on your senses, full-on. It was the soundtrack of Courtney Bryant's life. It was the rhythm she moved to during her nightly laps around the main casino floor.

By the time she turned fifteen, Courtney had started circulating around the gaming rooms, greeting guests and alerting pit bosses or security if she saw or sensed something untoward or unusual happening. She knew the games; she knew the rules. Mostly, she knew people. Her keen eye had helped apprehend would-be cheaters, and her intuitiveness had halted several altercations before they got out of hand.

Altercations. Conflicts. Fights. Like the one in the school hallway yesterday between Reign and Jake.

"Hey, tootsie, wanna come play with me?" A middle-aged man, a drink in each hand, accosted her by the blackjack tables. "With you nearby, I could get a flucky." He leered, undressing her with his eyes. "Want me to show you what that means?"

Courtney flashed him a courteous, professional smile. Get a flucky. How original. Translated from alcohol-fueled slurese, it meant "get off lucky." She told him, "Be a good boy, go find a flucky your own age."

Before dashing away, she tilted her chin up and eyed the nearest ceiling camera, just to make sure security kept tabs on the guy in case he decided to hassle someone else. The cameras in the casino kept everyone honest and, to her mind, safe. They gave Dan Bryant peace of mind. With his tacit encouragement, Courtney not only patrolled the casino floor, but had ramped up her involvement by keeping serious tabs on other hotels, who had state-of-the-art gaming equipment, who might be attracting the kind of hipster guests the Del cultivated.

Was Steve Wynn getting ahead of them? How could they cut Donald Trump off at the pass?

Dan's daughter knew her stuff. Which games gave the house the biggest advantage—roulette and slots were pretty much sucker's games—and which had odds only slightly in favor of the house, like craps.

She wasn't old enough to wager in public, but even in private, Courtney wasn't much of a gambler. The possibility of the big life-altering win held no allure for her. She already had everything she could ever want, or need.

Mostly.

For a split second, unbidden, Jake's warm eyes and soft smile appeared in front of her. She blinked hard, erased the image, and went about her business. A long-haired dude wearing shades and a blonde on each arm strode toward a Texas Hold 'Em table. One of the Killers, she realized, the local-rockers-made-good that Taryn was all over. And as long as they stay in that cool zone, they were totally welcome and courted at Delmonico's.

Lately, Dan Bryant leaned on her ever more heavily when it came to booking acts. He'd agreed with his daughter and her Girls that the Del would always top the other hotels as long as they kept booking the most raging rockers and rappers and sharp, political standups, and attracting the sharpest of hip young Hollywood.

Ever since Courtney entered her teens, and got involved, the Del had kicked Hard Rock butt, and whipped the Palms nine times out of ten. It was a tough act to keep up. Especially when Courtney had high school on her plate, college looming, her friends' crises to attend to, and now her own with Liam and Jake.

Another member of the Killers crossed her path, and shot

her a wink. She waved back, wishing Taryn were there to prompt her on their names.

Taryn! Oops, she totally owed Ted March, manager of the Bones, a call.

She stepped into a quiet alcove and punched in his number.

"Hi, Ted, Courtney Bryant from the Delmonico. We're so pysched that the guys will be performing here soon. I wanted to check in and see if there's anything special you need for them. I hear Fury likes to have a case of grape bubble gum backstage. Is there anything else you need?"

She was almost sorry she'd asked.

The list of perks the Bones demanded was so long that Courtney told Ted to email it to her. Then she got to her real reason for calling. "Some of our high rollers are asking for backstage passes, as well as entrée to the after-party. That's not a problem, right?"

It wasn't. Ebullient Ted said he could spare six passes, would that be enough? That was fine since she only really needed one—for Taryn. "Fabulous! Thanks so much. I'll be sure to look for your list. We're really looking forward to having the guys," she said. She was about to hang up, when Ted added that if any of the high rollers happened to be great-looking women, he could probably find more all-access passes. If she knew what he meant.

Oh, she knew all right.

She despised the backstage scenes at rock concerts, where groupies demeaned themselves for the sake of bragging rights to a hookup with any random ax-slinger. The more famous the better, of course. They didn't care if they got treated like so much disposable trash. Courtney shivered.

Taryn's agenda was different; she only wanted her music to be heard, to be appreciated by Fury, the group's lead singer. But would it matter in the end? By procuring the passes, was she throwing one of her Girls into a vicious lion's den?

All at once, Courtney needed alone time, craved her own space, needed to get upstairs and think. About Taryn. Liam. Reign. And damn it, Jake. She made for the express elevator to the penthouse. She didn't get there.

A cocktail waitress in a skimpy outfit came up to her in the alcove. "There's a man outside who wants to talk to you about booking a special event," she reported.

"Where's Bill Martin or Tanya?" Courtney asked.

"With other customers," the waitress replied.

Courtney sighed. "Okay. I'm on it." Reluctantly, she followed the waitress through the crowd, and went on autopilot when introduced to an older, nattily dressed Del patron, managing not to cough too much from his cigar smoke. Leading him to the catering office, she booked a cocktail party for his top ten tire salesmen and their guests on Delmonico's roof garden. When he left, she scribbled Bill Martin a note reserving the garden at the desired time.

Tired, Courtney leaned her head back in the chair for a moment. And there they were again, pictures she didn't want to see. Jake cupping her chin. Jake kissing her softly. Jake—arm in the air, about to come down on Reign. And another, earlier picture. Jake punching Liam.

So who was Jake Martinez? The boy she'd spent one afternoon with, a young man mourning the loss of his mother, ripped from his home, and dropped into a strange terrain. The boy who triggered a chemical reaction in her, a lust she'd never known. Was he just a lost kid, in need of a friend, a lover?

Or was he some common thug with a lucky biological connection to some Vegas high roller?

Didn't matter. Courtney had to cut him loose from her conscious, subconscious, and anywhere else he'd started to invade. She and Jake were a not-happenin' thing for any number of reasons. She just didn't know how exactly, to disconnect.

Her cell beeped and she discovered a text message from Taryn.

> **Any news on the passes? Pant. Pant. Pant.**
> **Got M,** she replied.
> **:-D :-) yaaaa-hooo!!!! mwah! U R Da Bomb!!!**
> **UR welcome.**
> **Listen! Hot off the presses—got it from Leesa, who got it from some saleschick, who got it from gossip-maven.com. Confirmed by Shelby—Reign's parents are splitsville, or will soon be. Gossipmaven's going live with the bombshell that some hot stud has come between them.**
> **Poor Reign!**
> **Yeah. Probably why she's been such a bee-atch lately.**
> **I thought it was because of Brad.**
> **That 2 probably. Sux! G2G.**
> **Bye.**

The unhappy news flash might explain Reign's uncharacteristically sulky moods and borderline violent behavior. Between Brad's rejection and betrayal, and the potential breakup of her parents, no wonder she's completely flipped out! What else could explain the way she'd hauled off and slapped Jake?

But it didn't explain Jake raising a hand back to her. Men who hit women were subhuman, animals, criminals as far as Courtney was concerned. There was no room for anyone like that in her life.

Standing, yawning, Courtney resolved to get upstairs. Then her eyes fell on a grid laid out on the desk. WORK SCHEDULE, it said. A quick perusal told her that Jake *was* scheduled to work that night, but not until later. He was probably in the staff quarters right now.

Her heart quickened. The staff quarters were located just behind the hotel. Courtney only went there during the holiday season, playing an elf to her dad's Santa Claus, dispersing gifts to the kids of the Del staff, then leading them all back into the hotel for an amazing party.

But it wasn't Christmas. She bore no gifts. She wasn't going there.

* * *

She headed down the corridor and turned into the main banquet hall. A banner strung across the room read: CONGRATS, SALLY JONES, SALESWOMAN OF THE YEAR. Catering waiters and busboys were setting up the room. She smiled at them as she crossed the room into the banquet hall kitchen. Waving quickly to the prep cooks who were slicing and dicing at their chop counters, she stepped out the back door into the alley.

Across the employee parking lot stood the simple, two-story, white stucco staff quarters. She was almost all the way across the parking lot when reason finally took hold of her. What was she doing? This was insanity!

She was about to do a 180, when the squeaky sound of the front door of the staff quarters stopped her in her tracks. She knew who it was before seeing him. Jake stepped out. His white waiter shirt was only half buttoned; it gleamed against his cocoa skin. His long dark hair, tucked behind his ears, glistened. Had he seen her from a window or was this coincidence?

"Courtney," he called to her softly.

She could have kicked herself. What was wrong with her? It shouldn't matter that she had been obsessed with him since day one. Jake had been about to bitch-slap Reign. End of story. She ought to get him fired, not come crawling to his bedroom. Which of course she wasn't doing!

"What are you doing back here?" Jake asked, walking toward her, "Slumming?"

She felt a flush of anger creep up her neck. Who was he to talk to her like that? She forced herself to complete the U-turn, and walk away from him. But she didn't get far.

He was by her side, in step with her. "Hey, look, I'm sorry. That was a stupid thing to say. And"—he touched her arm— "I was trying to find a way to tell you that I really feel bad about what happened in school with Reign."

"What *did* happen?" she asked pointedly.

"I don't exactly know. I never—I swear, never!—hit a woman, never even raised my hand to a chick."

"No, huh? But punching out guys, that's all right? You punched my . . ." She couldn't say "boyfriend." "You got into a fight at my party."

"Yo, that was different. That guy took a swing at me first. I don't back down," he defended himself.

"He was drunk," Courtney pointed out, remembering Liam's obnoxious behavior that night.

"So that makes it all right?" Jake challenged. "Richie Rich gets smashed, smacks a waiter around? And that's cool with you?"

No, it wasn't. Jake wasn't expecting her to answer.

"I'm not making excuses, but Reign went at me first, too. Going to hit her back, man, that was pure impulse. As soon as I realized what I was about to do, I stopped."

"Don't you mean *I* stopped you?" Courtney arched her eyebrows.

"I stopped myself. You clawing at my wrist was just a bonus. I still have scars."

"Reign shouldn't have slapped you," Courtney conceded. "She's been . . . sorta, going through some stuff. And I guess coming from a household full of actors, she can be over the top, a real drama queen."

"Boyfriend issues?" Jake guessed.

"That, and her parents might be having troubles, too. She hasn't told us herself, but that's what we're hearing."

"They are?" She was surprised by how keen Jake's interest seemed. "Are they divorcing?"

"I don't know. It'll probably work out," Courtney replied.

He stroked the side of her arm and, without intending too, she moved closer to him. In the next second, they were touching, hands, hips. And then they kissed. It hit her again, how soft his lips were, softer than she'd ever have imagined for a boy with such rough hands.

A car pulled into the lot and they sprang apart. A busboy hopped out, waved to Jake, and hurried toward the back entrance of the kitchen as the car pulled away.

Jake grabbed hold of her hand. "Come on."

As she climbed into his car, Courtney realized she didn't care where he was taking her. Being somewhere, anywhere, alone with Jake Martinez was exactly what she wanted.

Pulling out of the parking lot, he headed south on the Strip, but made a quick left onto a small side street. Courtney thought maybe he knew a back way to Lake Mead, or even Hoover Dam, but after a while, he turned down a dirt road and stopped the car. "Sometimes I just go out riding. I discovered this spot the other day, kinda liked it."

She could tell why. Considering that they were surrounded by desert, the area was unusually green. They got out and walked down a slight slope to where a narrow creek ran and sat beside one another.

For a while, no one spoke. Then Courtney surprised herself by blurting out, "You don't like Reign."

The subject caught him by surprise. "Reign del Castille? I barely know her. Except for her being extremely rude to me in school that day, I've never even talked to her."

"And yet," Courtney pointed out, "that day when you and I went to Lake Mead, at the café? You called her a pathetic, spoiled brat, desperate for attention, too impressed with herself to bother with other people."

Jake was amused. "Were you wired? Did you record what I said?"

Courtney blushed. The truth, that she replayed every moment she'd ever spent with him, over and over in her head, memorized his words, his gaze, his touch, so she'd know him by heart, was embarrassing. She skipped over it, went elsewhere. "You said the only way you could keep your promise to your mom was to go to Brighurst. How does that play out?"

"So now we're answering a question with another question, huh?" He continued to tease her.

"I just . . ." She paused. "I want to know about you. Is that a bad thing?"

"My parents weren't married," he said quietly, "possibly because my father was already married. I'm the result of a secret, passionate affair."

Courtney tingled at those words, but fought the feeling. "I'm taking it your biological father is someone of means?"

"He's rollin' in it, you got that right," Jake acknowledged. "My moms never wanted his money, not that I know if it was offered. She only asked one thing of him. That when it came time for college, he would pay. That was it. And that's probably how it would've played out, only she got cancer. And the day she got diagnosed, she contacted him and told him he had to step up because she wasn't going to be around anymore to handle things."

"Wow," Courtney murmured. His mother had made sure he'd be taken care of even while facing death. How completely unlike her own mother, who even today couldn't be bothered to find out how Courtney was doing. "Have you met him yet?" she asked. "I mean, obviously he lives around here, or you wouldn't be at Brighurst."

He nodded. "It was weird—he's a stranger yet he's my father."

"Who is he?" There, she'd said it. She held her breath.

Jake shook his head. "Can't say. I mean, I'm not gonna say. There's lots of reasons."

"Because," Courtney kidded, only slightly offended, "it's none of my business?"

Jake didn't laugh. "I like you, Courtney . . . in spite of, well, let's just say I wouldn't have expected to. And if I would tell anyone, I'd tell you. But it's not the right—"

"Time?" she interrupted.

"It's not the right *thing*," he corrected her. "It's not my place to blab someone's secret. Too many people might get hurt. And I don't want that on my head."

All at once, Courtney got it. Jake's father was married. Probably even had a family. A family who might not know about Jake, or accept him. A family who wouldn't want their dirty laundry aired. And Jake wasn't about to rat them out. If she could believe that, it'd make him a good guy, an honorable guy. Maybe he'd told the truth about the Reign encounter, that he would never have actually hit her.

"Could I ask one other question?"

"Knock yourself out." He shrugged.

"This father. He's paying for your tuition, and for college next year, right? So why are you working at Delmonico's? Why doesn't he just put you up at some hotel, or get you an apartment?"

Jake tugged a blade of grass out of the ground, twisted it around his fingers. "Look, my moms didn't want his money, and neither do I. I have no choice about being here in Vegas, or going to Brighurst. But after that, I can make my own way. I want to. And he, my father, was cool about it, probably makes it easier for him not to have me in his face. He pulled some strings to get me this job because I asked him to."

"My dad hired you?" she checked.

"Yeah. Dan Bryant did as a favor to my father or maybe it was a friend of my father's. I'm not sure. Anyway, I'm cool with the way it worked out—considering."

"Your mother loved you a lot, to make sure you'd be taken care of," Courtney said, trying to quell an unfamiliar lump in her throat.

"So," Jake said, "I showed you mine. Now you have to show me yours."

"Excuse me?" Courtney was taken aback.

He laughed. "Just an expression. I mean, I told you everything I could about myself. Now it's time for you to start answering some of my questions."

Courtney shrugged. "Bring it."

"Do you know why she left?" Jake asked. "Your moms?"

Okay, she hadn't expected him to go there. She'd already spilled all she wanted to about her mom. "I don't know why she bailed. My dad never said, so my best guess is he was fooling around. Isn't that the reason most couples split up?"

Jake's answer was to move closer to her, so close, their thighs touched. Slowly, he put his arm around her, and drew her to him. He cupped her chin. "I would never mess around, or split, if I had someone like you," he murmured.

The kiss was more intense than the one they'd shared at Lake Mead. It led to another. And another. And to falling back on the grass, wrapping themselves around one another, tasting, touching, stroking, and caressing as they rolled around. Jake was on top of her now, and she could feel his heart hammering in his chest. He wanted her. And she him, desperately, completely, and immediately. And it scared the shit out of her.

"What's wrong?" He pushed himself up on his palms.

She'd started to shake. "I don't know . . . nothing."

But she did know. She was about to open herself up to someone for the first time and she had no control over herself. This made no sense, whatever "this" was with Jake. And yet, it made ultimate sense. She wanted him to be part of her, to—what? Make her feel whole? How cheesy could you get?

"You're crying," he observed tenderly. "Do you want to stop?"

Quickly brushing tears from her eyes, she shook her head. No way could she speak.

She didn't have to. "I know," was all he said.

He moved slowly, exquisitely gently. With great tenderness, he lifted her shirt over her head and caressed her, with his hands, with his lips. She ran her hand up under his white shirt, and unbuttoned it.

Courtney had always known that when the moment came, when the time was right to give herself completely to someone, to let someone know her, be inside her, body and soul, she would know it.

She could never have imagined whom it would be with.

* * *

Courtney's world had shifted on its axis. Either that, or she existed in two realities, the rote familiarity of the everyday, and this new one. The one in which she was consumed by Jake Martinez. The one in which he occupied every waking thought, where she constructed fantasies, and he made them come true. The one in which she wondered how she'd ever lived without him.

Alt-reality was like imported dark chocolate, irresistibly rich and soul satisfying. Ultimately? Too much of it was very, very bad for you. At some point, she was going to have to break it off with Jake. But not yet.

No one could know. Obviously.

And not, she chided herself, because Jake happened to be working as a Delmonico's waiter. Not because he wasn't a Vegas designer-clad scene-maker. She wasn't ashamed to be seen with him, or any other rich girl/poor boy cliché. That happened in TV movies; this was real life. And as such, way more complicated.

Starting with: he wouldn't even tell her who his father was, who he really was. And ending with, she hadn't exactly broken it off with Liam. Yet.

So, no, her relationship with Jake had to fly under the radar. Way under.

Were she to tell one person . . . one of her Girls even? . . . it'd be the same as lighting up a billboard on the Strip. Word would get out so fast she'd get whiplash.

Courtney Bryant *spread* gossip; *she* wasn't the subject of it. No one could know that at school, she lived for the moments she and Jake would, accidentally on purpose, pass in the hallway. No one could interpret the darting, conspiratorial glances they exchanged, a tantalizing reminder of the romantic, tender, sexy secret they now shared.

It'd been two weeks, and they'd established a pattern. After school Courtney would get out of her limo, find her dad in the hotel and say hi, then cut out to the staff quarters parking lot where Jake would be waiting in his car. They'd take off for parts known, making love between the boulders above Hoover

Dam, on the shores around Lake Mead, by the unmarked scenic views of Red Rock National Conservation Area. Everywhere they discovered secluded areas to make out, private nooks and crannies where they could spend hours discovering every part of each other.

They explored parts heretofore unknown to Courtney. Valley of Fire State Park, Desert National Wildlife Refuge, where they ditched the car and hiked . . . until they found a private spot.

He'd refused her offer to come up to her suite, or go to any other hotel room in town. He'd turned down meals, catered or otherwise; he didn't care to visit any of Las Vegas's famous sights, though Courtney thought he might want to ride the roller coaster at the New York, New York hotel or check out the pyramid at the Luxor, maybe go to the top of the Eiffel Tower at the Paris Hotel. He did admit to a fascination with the water ballet outside the Bellagio, but seeing it once was enough. He wasn't interested in the clubs, the strip joints, or even just seeing the wedding chapels.

Jake was about nature, and nature was taking its course between him and Courtney.

* * *

The night they got busted, they'd lingered too long at Valley of Fire State Park, and then hit massive traffic getting back. Jake was late for work, so she'd gone straight to the employee parking lot with him. After one last hurried clutch, he departed for his dorm, she for the hotel.

Only to be intercepted at the big blue Dumpster in the alley outside the catering kitchen by Dan Bryant, who wore a sleek Armani suit and a tight-lipped frown.

Courtney's stomach seized. Nothing about the upcoming scenario was going to be pleasant.

"Dad! W-what are you . . . uh . . . why are you out here?" she stammered.

Former athlete, current hotel magnate Dan Bryant cut to the chase. "You're seeing that boy. The waiter."

The best defense, he'd taught her well, was a good offense. Courtney had several at the ready.

Your point?

Are you having me followed?

Have I been caught on tape? Caught in the act?

Her dad intercepted before she'd chosen which to go with. "Bill Martin told me, and some of the other staff have seen you leave and come back together. I saw you myself just now."

Okay, scratch denial. She'd been ratted out. What sucked was that she ought to have anticipated it, figured out a counterplay. She had only one play open to her: honesty. Courtney lifted her chin and looked directly into her dad's eyes. "Yes, Jake and I have been hanging out. Is that a problem?"

"No, but it's an embarrassment—to both of us."

Stealthed again! Of the arguments Dan might've trotted out, like 'why are you keeping secrets from me?' or some rule about a ban on employer/employee relationships, embarrassment was a dark horse.

"I'm shaming you, and myself?" She purposely made it sound worse.

"Yes, you are! Because I own this place and you are my daughter!"

"I can't believe you just said that!" she countered, her voice rising in outrage. Deep in his heart, Dan was a true egalitarian; he'd brought his only child up the same way.

"You're saying Jake isn't good enough for me?" she challenged. "That it's shameful for me, Courtney Bryant, to be going out with lowly Jake Martinez?"

"That's not the issue!" he barked.

"Then what is, Daddy?"

Dan didn't back down. "We could start with the fact that you kept this from me. Lying by omission is still a lie."

"Right back atcha, Dad. You lied to me, too," she said, quietly now. "You said Bill hired Jake, but we both know that's not true. *You* did. So what is it about Jake Martinez that you don't want me to know?"

Dan's solid, square jaw clenched, and his face reddened slightly. She'd struck a nerve. "It's just . . . complicated. And that's all I can say. You'll have to trust me. And you'll have to obey me. I forbid you to see Jake Martinez anymore. End of story."

With that, he turned back, disappearing through the kitchen door, leaving Courtney to wipe away tears that brimmed and threatened to splash over her lashes. It wasn't just her dad's outburst that stung. It was because a tiny part of her, the worst part of her, agreed with him.

* * *

When she returned to the penthouse she found an envelope on her bed. Inside was a message from her father. *Liam called. Wants you to call him back. I've left you complimentary vouchers to use at the Bellagio for dinner and dancing. Charge anything else to my account.*

Her first impulse was to shred the note and the vouchers,

refuse to be manipulated. Courtney rarely acted on her first impulse. Spinning situations to her advantage was her style, and the mention of Liam in the note brought one to mind.

She hadn't broken up with him yet. No matter what happened, or didn't happen, with Jake, the honorable thing was to cut Liam loose. Neither had ever been a random hookup; both deserved more from her.

Doing it over dinner at the Bellagio wasn't the worst possible way. At least, she thought with a rueful smile, he wouldn't be paying the bill for his own breakup dinner.

"Courtney!" The thrill in Liam's voice was unmistakable. "Babe, I've missed you."

She listened with only half an ear as he apologized for having been busy with daily lacrosse practices and getting hit hard with studying and frat responsibilities. She used to wonder what it would be like if you knew someone was headed for a train wreck, but they were blithely unsuspecting. Now she knew. It sucked.

They'd agreed to meet at Light, the posh Bellagio night spot, so Courtney could do some recon, checking on why the club had been getting so much press lately. It was also the place they'd be least likely to bump into anyone they knew. Their crowd, when not at the Del, was more likely at the hip-hopping Caramel, the Whiskey Bar, or Body English.

As her limo glided past the fabulous Bellagio's fountain in front of the spectacular hotel, she was surprised but relieved to feel her nerves calming. This evening, at least on the surface, was a return to "familiar." Even if she was only playing the role, it was a comfortable one, the socially in-control princess she had been before Jake turned everything upside down.

She'd aced stressful situations before. This was just one more. Wasn't it?

She spotted him in the lobby standing beside a large sign advertising the hotel's Cirque du Soleil show called *O,* one of the most popular attractions on the Strip. She and Liam had seen it together. They'd preferred it to the group's *Zumanity* performance over at New York, New York, which they'd also seen together, and had planned to see *KA,* the new one. So many memories, so many plans. She pushed them out of her mind as she approached him.

"Hey, babe," he greeted her with an unsuspecting, open smile.

"Hey." She pecked him lightly on the cheek.

"Is that all I get after not seeing you for two weeks?" he teased good-naturedly.

"I'm getting a cold," she lied. "I think the air conditioner is set too high in my bedroom."

"Speaking of your bedroom . . . ," Liam started, but she pretended she didn't hear him, sashaying over to the maitre d', who greeted her with a huge hug and led them over to a romantically lit cozy corner table.

They ordered grilled shrimp (for her), rack of lamb (for him), and a side of fries to share.

It was a code of honor among hotel owners: she, Dan Bryant's daughter, would not order liquor, a potentially embarrassing situation for the staff, which would either have to refuse her or risk breaking the law by serving her. Liam knew the drill, and followed suit. They asked for a bottle of Pellegrino water. Right after the waiter poured, she began her rehearsed speech.

"Liam, I've been thinking about us."

"Me, too," he said, with a sparkle in his eye.

Don't make this harder, she thought. "You know how I sort of flipped out the other day? When we were . . . you know, in my room? I led you to believe I was ready, and then suddenly, I stopped? I feel really badly about that—"

Liam reached over and closed his hand over hers. "Don't. It's okay."

"It's kind of not okay," she said, slipping her hand out from under his. "Maybe there's something wrong with me, but I'm not ready for real sex."

He winked. "Fake sex works . . . as long as it's with you."

She hadn't expected lighthearted teasing. "But you're nineteen," she reminded him, "nearly twenty. You have to be, you know, frustrated. Who wouldn't be?"

She'd hoped to draw him into an admission that he wanted to go all the way with her, that he'd hoped it would happen soon. And that if she told him it might be a long time comin', maybe he'd rethink their relationship. Maybe she'd get him to leave her.

Not so much.

"It's cool, Court," Liam insisted, "if that's all you're worried about. I mean, we have an amazing time when we mess around. You turn me on—more than any girl I've ever known. If you're not ready, then I'm not either. When it's right for you, it'll be right for both of us."

Damn him for being so . . . decent! And damn her for not anticipating he'd react like that.

"But what if it never happens?" she whispered.

Liam leaned back in the comfortably cushioned chair and

folded his arms. He looked, if anything, amused! "Are you try-ing to tell me maybe you're gay? 'Cause I don't buy that one, not for a second. I know you too well, I know your body too well. And I know how to turn you on."

Courtney colored. Gay? At this moment, she almost wished.

He leaned in close, took both her hands across the table now. "I know what's stopping you."

He did? "You do?" No, he couldn't know about Jake—

"You're all about trust. You're not a dime-a-dozen Vegas girl who'll hook up with just anyone. You need to trust a guy totally, with all your heart and soul. Someday I'll earn that trust, and then we'll take our relationship to the next level. You and me? We're in it for the long haul. I have faith in us."

This sucked! Why was Liam being so amazing?

"No," she pressed on, repeating that he was nearly twenty. "Men have needs," she reminded him. "A woman—not a girl—who'll satisfy him in every way. Who'll do the things that I"—her voice cracked, "won't."

"Well, I could always go to a hooker. It's legal here, you know."

Courtney's eyes widened. He was still making light of this.

"But you know I would never do that," Liam self-corrected. "I don't want anyone but you. In any way."

Pretending she hadn't heard him, she blurted out, "It's only fair to you that we break up."

The expression on his face nearly shattered her. He looked as if someone had hurled a bucket of ice water at him. "You're breaking up with me."

"It's the right thing to do," she said, her voice shaking.

"No it's not," he said urgently seeming to shake off his initial shock. "There's something else going on here. What did I do? Is it because I got drunk and out of line at your party last month? Whatever it was I'm sorry. I'll fix it. Just tell me what to do."

The thought that she was seeing someone else never crossed his mind. He continued, "You and me, Courtney?—we're cut from the same cloth. We're right for each other. I know it, and somewhere, deep inside, you know it, too."

She did.

Courtney wimped out. The only breaking to be done that night was in her secret heart.

Chapter 15

Flesh 'n' Bones

"And I know that my heart will go on . . ."

The plaintive wail of Céline Dion's signature ballad was a crowd-pleasing tearjerker to the multitudes who spent megabucks to see her Vegas show. To Taryn, it was more like the shrieking of a histrionic, breast-clutching shrew.

Although she and her parents socialized with Céline and her family, and Taryn genuinely liked the woman personally, she was not so much the fan of her music. She shared her titanic dislike of the schmaltzy tunes with her father, Ivan, but her pops was too much of a gentleman to ever admit it to anyone except Taryn. It was their secret.

Not so secretly, Courtney used to agree with Taryn's nose-scrunching Dion distaste. Their iPods were Céline-free zones.

Until recently, that is.

Now, in the express elevator together, going down from

Courtney's crib to the Delmonico Arena, Courtney was singing along with the Muzak! What up with that? Lately, her sista-friend seemed to have had a personality transplant. Once sharp, sardonic, smart, brutally quick-witted, and spin-controlling, Courtney had morphed into Ms. Mush, finding the corniest jokes hilarious, the hokiest songs . . . like . . . *good*. Paul McCartney called them "silly love songs," but, dude, this stuff was like Velveeta, authentic cheese product.

Courtney was all happy-go-sappy, and Taryn had not a guess why. It couldn't have had anything to do with the Jake Martinez file she'd traded for the Bones tickets, which was the only other un-Courtney act she'd witnessed in the last few weeks. Unless, it occurred to Taryn, Court and Liam had finally done the deed. But in Taryn's experience, hookups didn't result in this kind of drooling, short-bus-riding dopiness.

Unbearably, Céline caterwauled " . . . *and on . . . and on . . .*" until they reached the lobby level, on their way to the Delmonico Arena. It was three in the afternoon, and, sweet beans! the Bones—the real, live, and in the flesh BONES!!— were onstage, doing their afternoon sound check.

Courtney thankfully hadn't lost all her skills, and had arranged for Taryn to meet Monroe "Fury" Paige, in preparation for the after-party, which Taryn would attend, as a special guest of the Delmonico. This was the quiet moment, the one-on-one face time moment, before the storm that the after-party was likely to be. She knew she looked pretty cool, although her innards felt like a twisted coil of nerves.

Courtney flung open the double doors into the arena and marched confidently up the center aisle toward the stage. A deafening screech stopped them in their tracks.

"Yee-ow!" Taryn blurted, instinctively slapping her hands over her ears. She wasn't a squeal-of-reverb-on-the-mic virgin, but her eardrums had never been pierced quite like this before.

The next thing she heard was decidedly more excellent.

A deep, sexy male voice called out from the stage good-naturedly, "Obviously *that* has to come way down."

Fury was in front of them, center stage, his famously scratched Stratocaster guitar over his shoulder, signaling to the guy in the sound booth above them.

Taryn's excitement ramped up. He was wiry. He was scruffy in that sexy rock-star way. He was also unruffled and unfurious. Fury was everything she'd imagined, and more.

"Let's do this thing," she said, her throat suddenly dry. "Courtney, hook me up."

Only, pause. Courtney was not exactly ready to do this, or any other thing. Not without something from Taryn in exchange. She held her palm out.

"Give me your Sidekick first," Courtney said.

Taryn looked at her quizzically, not getting it.

"Give. It," Courtney repeated.

Taryn did as told.

Courtney punched in a number. "Okay," she said, handing it back, "I just put my number on speed dial one and hotel security on speed dial two. If you get into, or, knowing you, cause any trouble you cannot get out of safely—hit them both."

"Are you insane?" Taryn rolled her eyes, wishing her friend and benefactor would just get on with it: Make the damn intro!

Courtney took a deep breath. "I've really been struggling with this, Taryn, and I didn't know until right this minute what to do. As nice as Fury seems now—this is the sound check. Later, at the after-party, things will not be so mellow."

"Exactly what I was counting on," Taryn said with a grin.

Courtney was unamused. "The Bones have a rep when they're on the road. They travel with groupies, sleazy hangers-on, biker roadie types, and guys who are there just to supply them with drugs."

"Dude!" Taryn did a thumbs-up. "Sounds like my kind of people."

"Self-destruct much?" Courtney said.

"Paranoid much?" Taryn jested. "Besides, aren't you going to be glued to my side tonight, chaperoning, being your usual buzz-kill self?"

Courtney averted her eyes and lowered her voice, although no one even noticed the two girls at the back of the arena. "There's sort of been a change in plans. I have to go see someone."

"Who?" Taryn asked suspiciously, though not unhappily.

"Hotel stuff. Just remember: no matter where I am, I have your back," Courtney said quickly.

Taryn smiled. "Thanks, dudette, even if your concern is misplaced. The Bones are cool. I'm cool. I'll play for Fury, he'll totally get me. It's all good!"

Courtney bit her lip. "What are you wearing tonight?"

* * *

As Taryn had assured her preppy pal, she'd be dressed appropriately for the concert and the after-party. "No one in the band will even blink at my outfit. They'll think I'm total red state."

She'd chosen a studded black leather bra, leather pants with rawhide lace-up sides, and red-heeled boots with three-inch black platform heels, and had had the Delmonico stylist cut her bright red hair so that it spiked in every direction.

Her most brilliant stroke was the heart she'd drawn around her left eye, using thick black Stila eyeliner. The shape ballooned high over her eyebrow, and down along the corners of her eye, coming to a point just below her cheekbone. A lone teardrop, also rendered in black eyeliner, fell from the heart on her cheek.

Taryn had used makeup to symbolize what Fury's music meant to her. Dude, it did not get much cooler than that! She had a front row seat; Fury couldn't help but see her, and pick her out from the hordes of fans crowding the arena.

Now, her heart raced as the band hit the stage, amid their trademark ten-foot-high coiling tornados of diffused black smoke, whirling onto the stage from the wings. Fury himself leapt out of the center of the middle cyclone, his arm high in the air, poised to come down hard on the guitar. The arena, packed with Goths and metal-heads, biker boys, an entire tattoo crew—not one of the dorky preps from Brighurst was here—erupted into a blistering welcome of hoots, shouts, and whistles.

The Bones delivered.

The machine-gun drumbeats pounded, the bass guitar licks screamed, the keyboard slammed, and Fury launched into a Bones set of screamo rock, loud, raw, emotional, ripped from the gut. Intense.

For the next ninety scintillating minutes the Bones kicked ass, had the audience pumping fists, rambunctiously dancing, shouting the rapid-fire chants and lyrics along with the band—the only thing missing was a mosh pit, but Dan Bryant had drawn the line at that. Which was sort of a bummer, but it worked in Taryn's favor. Her first-row seat put her right in Fury's line of vision.

Eye contact was totally made, repeatedly during the show. For that, she had Courtney to thank. Her girl had made good on the promise. During the sound check earlier that afternoon, she'd been introduced to the entire band: the heavily tattooed, bald drummer, Sweat; the black-clad skinny Goth bassist, X, who had Kohl-rimmed eyes and a metal spike through his lip; and the keyboardist, Steve Z, who never took off his black shades.

With his scruffy clothes, long choppy hair, and day's worth of beard, lead singer/guitarist Fury was the one with the looks and the real talent.

He greeted them cheerfully. "You're the blonde, so you must be Courtney, the one I must Court—the owner's daughter."

Courtney tilted her head slightly and extended her hand. "I am, and yes, it'd be good if you did."

Fury smiled. "Manager Ted said you'd be by. Who's your cute friend?"

Taryn melted. Her stomach churned. The phrase "like buttuh," melting and churning at the same time, came to her, and she had to stifle a giggle.

"This is my Girl Taryn. She's an amazing singer, songwriter, and guitarist," Courtney answered, launching into her promo pitch.

Fury regarded her, his eyebrows arched. "Is that so?"

Taryn blurted out, "I think you guys are the only ones

worth listening to right now. You have something to say *and* you really rock."

"All right!" Fury cheered, pumping his fist in the air. "A woman with taste. Maybe we can hear *your* music some time."

"How about now?" Courtney seized the moment.

Taryn's heart flipped like a fish out of water, but she held tight to her cool.

"Wish I could," Fury said with genuine disappointment, "but we got started late on the sound check, and as you might've heard, things aren't going as smoothly as we'd hoped. So we need to be here for a while. Then we've gotta prep for the show tonight."

"Well," Courtney said, her forefinger to her lips, "Taryn will be coming to the after-party. You *could* listen to her music then. I mean"—she winked—"before you get too wasted?"

Fury threw his head back and laughed. "Good one, owner's daughter."

"Seriously," Courtney said, "I'd consider it a personal favor."

Slyly, Taryn kicked her ankle, and Courtney amended, "Truth is, once you hear her, it'll be the Delmonico that did you the favor."

"You've intrigued me, Courtney-owner's-daughter," Fury said with a mischievous grin. "Both of you."

To her horror, Taryn blushed. "I won't take long, I'll just do some guitar licks, a couple riffs and lyrics and . . ." She stumbled.

Fury assured her, "Take as long as you need, Taryn—great name, by the way, like 'Taryn up the town.' Brilliant music can't be rushed. And I do solemnly swear"—this he said to Courtney—"I will not be trashed, wasted, hammered, stoned, or in a compromised zone while I have the pleasure of listening to Taryn's music. How's that?"

The dude was a charmer. Even jaded Courtney, who'd seen and heard it all, was down with him. They shook hands.

Fury asked, "Will you be at the party?"

Too quickly, Courtney shook her head. "I wish, but responsibility beckons, and I have elsewhere to be. Catch ya next time. Remember"—she shook a finger at him—"play nice with my Girl Taryn."

Fury had laughed.

It only hit Taryn later, when she'd come down ("offa my cloud," as the Rolling Stones sang), that Courtney was lying. That crap about the hotel business, and having somewhere else to be? Bull. Courtney had kept many secrets *for* her Girls. Now, it seemed she had one of her own, and was keeping it *from* them.

* * *

When the concert ended, two encores later, Taryn was dripping in sweat.

In just a few minutes, she'd be going up to their suite, to the after-party, where she'd play for them, and connect with Fury. Her life would be set. He'd hook her up with a record company, maybe she'd even play backup for him! No matter what, the whole Juilliard thing would never be brought up again. Even her father, the great Ivan Krakowski, would understand what Taryn had to do, and would do.

Taryn breathed deeply to steady her nerves as she picked up her guitar behind the concierge desk and walked through the lobby toward the elevator up to the private suite that the

Bones had commandeered for the after-party. It was hard to hang on to her ballsy-chick façade when her knees threatened to buckle beneath her. And it didn't help that security, in the form of three large, bald, intimidating bouncer types, stood, arms crossed, guarding the suite.

They stared down at her.

Gamely, she shoved her right boob up at them—the one she'd stuck the all-access pass onto.

Without expression, they opened the doors for her.

Taryn's heart slammed into her breastbone as she entered the suite—dude, it hadn't taken the band and their hangers-on very long to get the after-party going. The music blasted, drinks flowed, food abounded. Amid the usual caviar, sushi, sashimi, baby lamb chops, etc., Taryn noted the sardine and tomato sandwiches she'd read that Steve Z insisted be provided to him at every show.

The bar was blow-out Delmonico: fully stocked with top-shelf imported liquors and mixers. It struck Taryn that for a band whose music and entire vibe was about the angry, disenfranchised outsiders, the Bones were all about the Benjamins offstage. Demanding to be served with only top-flight everything.

She pushed the word "hypocrite" away, as she stared at the partygoers and tried not to be scared out of her wits. The room was filled with the kinds of people Courtney had described, a cornucopia of tattered leather types with explicitly raunchy tattoos—the biker contingent, was her guess. The rest were a true mash-up of grungy rockers, roadies, bodyguards, coked-out suits who must have been the managers and agents. This being Vegas, there was also a complimentary cache of leggy, scantily clad showgirls.

Taryn used her guitar as a shield to make her way around the suite, in search of Fury. When she spotted him, a tall *Playboy* type had a bare arm draped around his shoulder. He seemed to barely notice her as he was otherwise occupied: pouring himself a whiskey and gulping it in a straight shot.

As she made her way toward him, Taryn sniffed the air—a sweet, familiar aroma was emanating from a spot nearby: someone was smoking weed.

Okay, she was beginning to feel less anxious. She could be part of this.

At a couch behind a coffee table, X sat with Sweat and a couple of blondes who were spilling out of their short, tight dresses. A tall, very thin guy in dark glasses, a black T-shirt, and leather pants knelt beside the coffee table. He was cutting into a mound of white powder, forming it into lines on the table with a straight-edge razor.

Cocaine. Not Taryn's drug of choice. It frightened her.

Steve Z used a rolled-up dollar bill to snort a line of the coke, then strolled over to Taryn. "Hey, pixie, I remember you from sound check—saw ya at the show. What'd you think of it?"

Taryn grinned. "You guys were awesome."

Steve nodded toward the cocaine. "Want some? Eric always gets us the primo stuff." He nodded toward the skinny supplier with the razor.

"I'll pass." She gripped her guitar, sort of shoved it at him, as if to say, *this is what I'm here for.*

"Oh yeah, that's right! So let's hear what you can do," he said. "Plug in over there by the bar."

Taryn took a deep breath, and let Steve lead her over

toward the bar. She'd wanted Fury as her audience—but this was her moment to seize, and nothing would stop her. He helped her plug in. She settled on a bar stool, put her Bulga tassle hobo bag down by her feet, and launched into "Assassin Heart."

She was on the bridge when Fury materialized. Right in front of her, holding a drink, listening intently. X and Sweat gazed up at her with coke-brightened eyes, but she'd gotten their attention. Steve Z nodded approvingly as she ripped into the second verse.

Sweet beans! The expressions on their faces, their bodies moving along with her music, that was all the validation Taryn needed. She was in! This was the beginning of . . . of everything. Her real life—the life she'd been born for—was about to start.

Without even a break for applause, she segued into another original song, "Cursed." It was slower than "Assassin Heart," but its wrenching lyrics kept the band riveted. The rest of the partygoers, the dangerous dudes, skanky chicks, drug dealers, and suits, seemed to fade away: she was playing for the Bones, and the Bones were all about her music. It was all she wanted, and it gave her tacit permission to get deeper into her own real rock zone. She leaned over her instrument, closed her eyes, and became one with it.

She could feel Fury coming toward her. She didn't need to open her eyes; she knew his fingers were tracing the heart she'd drawn around her eye, his lips brushing her forehead. He whispered, "It's in your heart."

Taryn glowed. And kept on playing.

It was midway through "I'll Show You Mine," her fourth

song, that she opened her eyes, and realized—what the fuck?—
Fury wasn't there anymore. X and Sweat were also gone, as
were their showgirls. Steve Z had his back turned and was
walking away.

"Hey!" she yelled out to the keyboardist's back.

He swung around. A bottle of Jim Beam was in his hand,
and he shrugged. "Excellent music, pixie girl, but we gotta
jump."

Taryn refused to be bummed. They'd heard enough, she
surmised, to know she was amazing. Tomorrow she'd hear
from them, from Fury.

The suite was still packed with people, so she kept on playing. One of them might just tell Fury how kick-ass she was
after he left. Taryn launched into the hardest-rocking song in
her repertoire. She threw herself into it, shutting out everything but the song.

When she was done, the only sound in the room was that
of applause: by a lone set of hands. It was Eric, the guy whose
main job was scoring blow for the band. Other that that, the
suite was empty! Was there a fire drill she hadn't heard?

Eric crossed the room to her. "You are one hot little chick.
The way you sing really turns me on."

"Well, I sure know how to clear a room," she joked to
cover her mounting panic and dismay.

Eric went to reassure her. "It wasn't personal. The band's
on a tight schedule. They're only in town for a coupla days,
and they have other hot spots to hit, clubs, strip shows. This
was just the first pit stop of a very long night for them."

"Oh," was all Taryn could manage, chastising herself for
not realizing the Bones would make the most of a Vegas stay.

Probably they'd have invited her, too, had she not been so en-grossed in her music. Oh, well, at least they'd heard her before they'd gotten too hammered. Fury had made good on his promise.

Eric was talking. ". . . I told the roadies to split, too, if they ever wanted to see any good blow again on this tour."

"Why?" she asked, unplugging her guitar and picking up her Bulga tassle hobo bag.

"Why do you think?"

The leer in his voice tripped her inner alarm. She glared at him: this skeeve was like, undressing her with his glistening, drugged stare. He turned to the bar and poured out a tum-blerfull of whiskey. "I held back the best blow for us to share," he said, taking a clear bag of powder from his back pocket. "This stuff will blow your boots off—and then you can blow mine."

"I don't think so," Taryn scoffed, sounding tough to mask her fear. This asshole was flying on coke and booze. He wasn't gonna be dissuaded so easily. Her exit strategy was the door—she headed toward it.

Not quickly enough.

Eric the Ugly caught her under her upper arm, lifting her onto her toes. His grip was hard, viselike. "Don't leave with-out having a toot." It was not a request.

The wheels in her head spun, and for once, she was glad she was sober. Placating this drugged-out jerk would give her enough time to leave. "All right," she agreed. She followed him to the couch, where the coffee table was still covered in coke.

"Forget that shit," he said, nodding at the cocaine on the

table. "The stuff I have in my pocket will make you forget your name."

"On second thought"—Taryn grabbed her bag, started to stand up—"maybe another time. I have to go."

He pulled her back down onto the couch. "No, you don't." He pushed her down and yanked at her leather bra. "You're coming across, you little tease."

Before she knew what was happening, his cold hand was under the fishnet shirt, inside her bra, squeezing, his groin pressing urgently into her side.

Her bag slipped from her shoulder and scattered on the ground—cash, credit cards, her camera phone, her Sidekick. He looked down, bleary-eyed, and laughed. "All your toys. Well, they won't help you now."

Her wits, and compact body, would, however. With all her might, she pulled away and rolled out from under him, scrambling to her feet. She grabbed at her Sidekick, and hit 1. Before she could hit 2 for hotel security, he had reached out from his prone position on the couch and grabbed her boot at the ankle.

The next thing she knew she hit the ground, banging onto her back with a painful *thud*. Instantly he was on her, pinning her arms down above her head with one hand and pulling at the band of her pants with the other. She tried to kick, but he was sitting on her legs. "Get off me, you fucking asshole!" she shouted, desperately trying to get at her Sidekick.

"Scream some more," he challenged her in a mocking tone. "These rooms are soundproof—the Bones demanded it."

Pitching back and forth, she thrashed violently but he was so much bigger she couldn't throw him off. Fueled on coke, he violently ripped her bra off, then went for her pants. Before she knew what was happening, Taryn was completely naked.

"No! Stop!" She screamed, kicked, pulled at his hair, even bit him, but he was too stoned to notice. He was a predator, and she, his helpless prey. She crossed her legs . . . and for the first time in her life, prayed.

No one heard.

His pants were off now—he hadn't bothered with his shirt— and he was tugging her legs, trying to pull them apart.

And then, he flew up into the air. Off of her. And he was screaming in pain.

Courtney, the most beautiful angel Taryn had ever seen, was beside her, covering her with a blanket hastily ripped off the bed, pulling her up, hugging her, shielding her.

A guy—in her hysteria, Taryn didn't realize who it was— was pounding the crap out of her attacker. She tried to tell Courtney what had happened, but heaving sobs wracked her small frame, blocked her words.

"It's okay, you're okay," Courtney kept repeating. "It's gonna be okay. Security is on the way. I called the police, too. Told them I'd take care of you, no need to call your parents."

Wrapped in Courtney's comforting arms, Taryn slowly began to calm down. Enough, at least, to witness the bashing Eric was getting, and realize who was delivering it.

"Jake," Courtney called, distressed, "that's enough! I want to kill him, too, but you can't. Don't."

Chapter 16

Danger, Courtney Robinson Bryant!

On the ride home in the limo, Courtney held Taryn tightly. Through her hiccupy tears and shaking, Taryn had managed to assure Courtney that she was okay, there was no need to go to the hospital. They'd gotten there just in time; she was bruised, but not battered, not, in the end, raped.

Nothing Taryn said could assuage her guilt: Courtney had fucked up, big time. She'd known better than to leave Taryn alone with the Bones. She'd known the scene would devolve into debauchery and danger. So she'd programmed in a speed-dial panic button?

Not good enough.

She had chosen being with Jake over protecting someone who'd been her friend all her life. And that sucked. Courtney was ashamed of herself.

"I'm so sorry, Taryn. This was all my fault."

Taryn gruffly pulled away from Courtney and scowled. "I put myself in this position. And they did listen to my music. They did! Before they left . . ." She trailed off.

Courtney grimaced. "It shouldn't have happened like that."

Taryn insisted, "Anyway, you wouldn't have been able to stop me if you tried."

"But I didn't," Courtney said ruefully, "I didn't try at all."

"Because you wanted to be with him? With Jake?" Taryn said softly, sniffling.

Lips pursed, Courtney nodded.

"It's okay," Taryn said. "You can tell me."

"I've been . . . seeing him," Courtney revealed. At the very least she owed Taryn the truth. "On the sly."

Of all things, *this* made Taryn grin. And the sight of a curly-lipped, smiling Taryn, her makeup one huge shmush all over her face, somehow cheered Courtney.

"So," Taryn asked, when Courtney had told her the whole story, "no one knows, not even Leesa and Reign?"

"No one."

"And . . . Liam?" Taryn asked cautiously.

Courtney groaned. "Liam doesn't know. He still thinks I'm, you know, with him. Luckily, lacrosse season is in full swing, and he's completely absorbed."

"Oh, Courtney," Taryn teased, "don't you know the old line? It's a tangled web we weave when first we practice to deceive."

"Yeah, well, you should know," Courtney retorted, then caught herself. "I'm just confused," she confessed. "Liam's a great guy. He's the one I should be with, but there's just no connection. Not on my part, anyway."

"You can't force yourself to be into someone you're not," Taryn said sagely. "You don't want to hurt Liam, but Jake shakes your wild thing, you gotta break it off with Liam. Leading him on is the only thing wrong with this whole scenario."

"Thanks, Yoda."

Taryn balled up a pretend fist. "Was that a short joke?"

They both laughed a hearty, tension-relieving laugh.

Then Taryn asked coyly, "So Jake . . . he's hot, huh?"

Courtney grinned. "Scorching."

She wouldn't spill every detail, but she would, and did, savor each and every one. Each and every time they'd hooked up, since that first time on the grass by the stream, when she'd cried, Courtney and Jake had gotten wilder, more fevered, more desperate for each other. It was like an addiction: you got a taste, and all you could think about was getting more, and getting more sooner. And more often.

They got reckless, seizing any opportunity, any place for getting together. They'd probably scored all over the Strip, in places she'd never dreamed of! Like in the bathroom of the downtown bus station and in the basement of school, in one of the hotel's storage closets, her back against a wall of brooms, her clothing at her feet, in his room at the staff quarters— that was really taking a chance!—they'd even found a secluded corner where they could watch the fountains at the Bellagio do their water ballet.

So far, the only place off-limits—a rule imposed by Jake— was up in her penthouse. He gave no reason beyond not being comfortable up there. Maybe his first time there, in the Sky Box Lounge at her party, had turned him off.

Courtney knew enough not to push him. But more and more, she wanted him beneath the soft Frette sheets of her humongous bed; she wanted him in the Jacuzzi with her; she wanted to show him pictures, play CD mixes for him on her rockin sound system, fit him into her life. Soon, she promised herself, she would come clean with her Girls, with Reign, and with Leesa. And eventually, with her dad. But if Jake refused to even come to her apartment—maybe that was a sign that it was still too soon.

He also refused her offers to go to clubs or swanky restaurants or even to see cool shows. On his waiter's pay, Jake couldn't afford luxuries. He refused to take money from his real father—or divulge his identity—and he would not allow Courtney to spend any on him. He wanted only one thing from her, and she freely gave it.

She stayed with Taryn all the way to the front door of the Krakowski mansion. "Are you going to tell your parents the truth?"

"I don't know—all I want to do is sleep."

"Taryn . . . it's time maybe you dialed it down. Y'know, you've been pushing really hard, going to seedy clubs, pretending to be part of a lifestyle that—"

"That what? I don't belong in? That says my music is meaningless?"

"I didn't say that, honey." Courtney tried to be gentle with her badly bruised buddy. "You're letting yourself in for a world of hurt, and maybe there's another way to get what you want."

"You think if I tell my parents, they won't force me to go to Juilliard and give up this stupid dream? Is that what you think is the right thing to do?"

"No!" Courtney contested hotly. "You know I'm on your side. But you nearly got raped tonight, Taryn! Come on, there's got to be another way to do the music you want without stepping off the goddamn edge every time. Maybe your parents . . . your father . . . maybe there's a way to get them to understand that. To understand you."

"Like Dan Bryant understands you?" Taryn challenged. "If you really believe I should confide in my pops, you wouldn't be hiding your little secret from yours."

Nailed.

"So here's the thing, Courtney. I'll keep your secret, but you gotta promise to keep mine.

"And hey, thank your hero boyfriend for me," she said before slipping inside the house.

* * *

It was late, well past 3 A.M. when Courtney got back to the hotel. She wasn't the least bit tired, and as it turned out, neither was Jake. He'd made a key for her, but tonight, he'd left the door unlocked. He was on the bed, shirtless. He'd known she'd come. The smallness, and plainness, of the room, in contrast to the opulence of her suite, always struck her when she was here. It was wonderful: a dim, quiet space where only the two of them existed. "Is Taryn all right?" he asked anxiously, bolting up on the bed.

"Thanks to you," she replied. "You were great."

"I hate guys like that," he growled. "Fuckin' drug dealers.

My moms would be turning in her grave. She thought she sent me away from all that, but here it is, in the land of hedonism at its height. Funny how people with too much money get into the same shit as people with no money."

Jake's whole body shook with emotion. Was it pure hatred for Las Vegas, still? Or a reminder of the dark side of his life before he got here? Before her?

She sat down on the creaking bed, and took his hand. "You were wonderful today," she whispered, kissing him. "You have no idea how much I love you."

"Yes, I do," he said, bending her back on the bed as he brushed a strand of hair from her face. "I know because it's how I feel about you."

* * *

Maybe it started that night. Or maybe they'd been taking tiny steps toward opening up to each other all along. After the Taryn rescue, their relationship deepened. Courtney shocked herself by telling him things she'd hardly ever admitted to herself, let alone talked about. Jake had asked if she felt pressure, having to help run the Delmonico. She was only seventeen years old.

She admitted that she did.

"But you're gonna go to business school, then, and eventually run the place on your own?"

Courtney squirmed. She didn't know what she wanted to do after high school. There was a part of her that never wanted high school to end!

She didn't love a lot of things about running the hotel. There was pressure to keep up, to glad-hand the high rollers, back up the staff setting up parties and events. And Dan relied on her to have her finger on the pulse of young Vegas: to know who and what was cool, cutting edge, hip and happening. Sometimes? She got tired of the responsibility. She looked back fondly on the days when she was just simply Daddy's little girl, not Daddy's go-to girl.

Jake had encircled her in his arms right then, kissed her tenderly. "Maybe you should talk to him," he said, "tell him how you feel."

Courtney laughed. Exactly the same advice she'd given to Taryn, who'd never follow it, either.

She confessed to Jake that Liam still thought they were together. Jake had actually been down with it—saying, in essence, it would throw Dan Bryant off their trail. Which was a spin Courtney should have thought of.

Jake began to answer her questions with more candor, too. He'd been one spunky little kid, the apple of his mother's eye. "To be honest? I didn't know we were poor or anything," he admitted. "I was cool with our small apartment, I had friends, we did stuff. Sure, I mean, there were, like, video games and things I wanted that I couldn't have . . . well, I couldn't buy."

"So you stole?" Courtney asked.

"Nah, I was more afraid of my moms than the cops! We just ended up getting pirated versions of games, movies, that kind of thing. It was cool."

The one not-so-cool thing about Jake's childhood was his lack of a father. He claimed not to have cared, but admitted that some kids called him a bastard, since his parents never married. "They could call me whatever they wanted," he told her, "but if one of them started on my moms, calling her names, watch out."

So he wasn't, she realized, by nature a fighter. He wasn't someone who always threw a punch first, and thought about it later. He'd grown up having to defend himself, and his family. It made a world of sense.

Jake talked so much about his mom, that over the next few weeks, Courtney felt she'd known Rosa Martinez, and mourned her loss. Until Jake wondered, "Yo, maybe it's your own mom you miss."

"That's where you're wrong, my sexy young friend . . . I have everything I need. There's only one thing I want, and only you can give it to me."

He peered into her eyes quizzically, wondering what it could be.

* * *

Courtney scurried around her apartment excitedly. Finally! She'd talked Jake into coming up to see her in the penthouse. Everything had to work, meaning: not too showy—she didn't want him to be put off by an ostentatious show of luxury, although that would be pretty hard to avoid.

She was going for sweet romance, not suite decadence.

Her dad was out of town on business, far enough way so there was little danger of him popping in on them. Which was one of the reasons Jake had agreed to tonight. He didn't want Dan Bryant to discover them in a compromising position either!

So they had the night. After all the down and dirty fun on the run they'd been enjoying, she wanted this night to be leisurely and sensuous.

She lowered the dimmer on all the lights and lit candles in a trail leading to her bedroom. A bottle of Cristal was chilling in the fridge and she wore a new pink satin bra and thong under a short, matching pink robe.

When Jake arrived he wore a wary expression. "Don't worry, we won't be able to do this often," she assured him, taking his hand and leading him along the trail of lit candles. "Since my dad's away it would be a shame not to enjoy the privacy. Besides, you have to admit it's better than a storage closet."

"I don't know," he insisted stubbornly. "I thought making it in the closet was pretty exciting."

"That's true," she allowed. "But right now we have time, something we don't usually have."

"Time," he repeated. "You're right. Time is a luxury."

In her bedroom, he peeled her robe off and they fell onto the bed. "God, you're gorgeous," he murmured as he ran his hands all over her body, pressing in all the right places. She used her teeth along his neck, biting him gently, tantalizing him by nibbling on his ear until they were both in a frenzy.

When they were done, they rested, drank the champagne, and tore apart a five-pound cold lobster she'd ordered up from the Lakers Lounge. "Just this once," he insisted, seeming to enjoy it all despite his words.

The lobster was messy and they went into the shower to wash it off. The sensuality of the hot, pounding water inspired them to go at it again, lathering one another with slow, caressing strokes.

Courtney came out of the shower before Jake and wrapped herself in a bath towel. As she stepped out into her bedroom, she stopped short.

There was someone in the doorway, wearing a megawatt

smile and carrying a bouquet of flowers. His mouth was moving, he was talking. But Courtney only caught a couple of words, like a cell phone, going in and out. "Your dad . . . wanted me to check on you. You knew . . . candles . . . getting prepared . . . for me."

Liam.

Chapter 17

Jilted Boyfriend Cries on Fashion Diva's Shoulder, Ruins Her New Dress

Shel-Chiced: She dumped him! You heard it here first . . .

Fashion Diva: No way! You're spreading false rumors again!

Shel-Chiced: I'm giving you the scoop, friend to friend. It'll be all over my mom's column tomorrow. But just wait'll you find out how it happened. He caught her in the act with—

Fashion Diva: Well?

Shel-Chiced: I can't say too much. But . . . here's a tease. He's low class. As in, just off the olive truck.

Fashion Diva: I don't know what you're talking about. What does he look like?

Shel-Chiced: K-Fed before the cleanup. Oops, I did it again . . . spilled too much of Mom's scoop. Better go.

When it all breaks loose tomorrow, remember who told you first.

Better get a pooper-scooper for that stanky gossip, Leesa thought angrily. Because it was all bullshit. She would not believe for one moment that Shelby had any real dirt on Courtney. No way would Courtney have kicked Liam to the curb. Not without telling her Girls!

Leesa had worked herself up into a righteous rage by the time she called an emergency meeting between herself and Reign and Taryn. They'd get to the bottom of this, and bail Courtney out. She'd called Reign, and texted Taryn, who wasn't picking up her cell phone these days. She hoped they'd both show up.

She'd chosen to meet at Ah Sin, an upscale Asian eatery inside the Paris Hotel. She didn't want to run into Courtney—not yet, anyway. And Ah Sin met all their requirements: it was chic, it was dark, and it served Pan-Asian cuisine for her and sweet, sugary French desserts for Reign and Taryn. When the host handed her a single red rose, she was confused.

"What's this for?"

"It's our policy, mademoiselle. You've been here before, no?" Oh, that's right, Leesa remembered. All females who entered the dimly lit eatery were greeted like this. "Thanks," she said, twirling the thornless rose in her hand. "I see my friend across the room."

"Yes, your friend Ms. del Castille is right this way." He led her to where Reign sat in a curtained booth along the far wall, wearing a disgruntled expression, her red rose tossed disdainfully on the cushioned banquette.

Leesa momentarily let go of her Shelby rumor rage as she became aware of male eyes following her progress through the restaurant. Was her pink Roberto Cavalli sundress cut too low, and was it even pulling along the butt? She slid quickly into the booth. "Do you think we can pull these curtains all the way around us?"

"Why?" Reign asked. "Are we going to pass government secrets, or is this just a run-of-the-mill drug deal?"

"No, I just suddenly hate the way I look in this dress," she whispered. "I felt like all the men in the room were staring at my boobs and ass."

"Your point?"

"It means I'm busting out of the dress," Leesa insisted.

"You *are* busting out of the dress," Reign pointed out. "In a good way! For such a fashion savant, you're completely patzo when it comes to your own body."

"What's patzo?" Was that another reference she didn't get?

Reign rolled her eyes. "Forget it, I made it up. The point is, I'd kill to look like you. Booty-licious may not be *Vogue*-alicious but it's what guys like. Walk past any newsstand and check the men's magazines if you want proof."

"I don't want to look like those women," Leesa insisted, not cheered by Reign's remarks. "It's . . . embarrassing. I wish I could puke it all up like Shelby does, but I can't make myself do it. It's too disgusting. I just wish I was rail thin like Courtney."

"Whatever. Suit yourself, Armani," Reign said as the waiter approached. They ordered garlic noodles and sushi, iced tea for Leesa. They tried sake for Reign, but no go, here at the Paris, they wouldn't serve her liquor. She settled, grumpily, for a Coke.

This wasn't the first time Leesa had noticed the chill in the air from Reign when she talked about Courtney. Now, the mere mention of Courtney's name had annoyed Reign. What was going on between them?

Well, Reign would have to deal, because Leesa wasn't going to wait any longer to spill Shelby's slimy gossip. 'Cause no way could she be right, and Reign would verify. When Taryn got here, the three of them would figure out a way to stop the vicious rumor before it got out. For once, *they'd* be helping Courtney.

"I have something upsetting to tell you," Leesa began.

"Bring it. 'Cause that's what I need—more upsetting news."

"Shelby said Courtney broke up with Liam. She's going to spread that phony rumor all over town! What should we do?"

Reign's face tightened into a fist. She spat, "We should break her arm, that's what we should do."

Leesa choked on her iced tea, totally spitting it up.

"I didn't hear you right, did I?"

"Oh, yeah you did."

Whatever was going on between Courtney and Reign was way worse than Leesa could have imagined.

"You did what?" Taryn tore into the booth, and plopped herself down, forcing Leesa to scooch over. "Why did you call me here? And, sidebar, why do you both look so . . . weird?"

Coming from someone dressed like Taryn, in ripped Nick & Nora pajamas and thwacky no-name thongs, that last question would've been funny if the convo wasn't so serious. Still, Leesa couldn't help but remark, "You do know that even punk rockers are so over grunge and that indie crap of looking like everyone else? That you can, in fact, be pretty in punk, if you'd just take my advice—"

"Off topic!" Taryn broke in. "You said this was a dire emergency. I don't think it's to discuss my couture. Straight up, why are we here?"

"Courtney dumped Liam, because she's found someone who floats her boat a little more often," Reign announced bitterly.

Taryn went from pissed to panicked in record time. "Who? I mean, how do you know?"

"Shelby text-messaged me . . . she said Courtney's with some person of a low class."

Now Reign's eyes narrowed suspiciously.

Taryn prodded, "What else did she say? Did she give a name, serial number, description?"

Leesa tried to remember how Shelby had responded when she'd asked what the guy looked like. "Oh, yeah, something I didn't get. About KMart? Or FedEx? Wait, I remember: she said Courtney's new guy looks like . . . 'K-Fed before the cleanup.' Whatever that means."

Taryn looked stricken.

Reign roared with laughter. "That's a good one—even though it's the biggest crock going."

"What does it mean?" Leesa asked.

"It's shorthand for Kevin Federline, that grungy guy Britney Spears married, then cleaned up for some magazine layout. K-Fed, like J. Lo? Get it now, Einstein?"

Leesa stuck her chin out. "You don't have to be like that, Reign. Not everyone gets showbiz shorthand. It doesn't mean I'm stupid."

"Well, don't get your La Perlas in a knot, 'cause it's all a crock of shit anyway," Reign retorted.

Leesa heaved a sigh of relief. "So it's not true; Courtney didn't break up with Liam. I just knew it. I'm going to call her now, and tell her that Shelby's about to spread dirt. She'll know how to nip it in the bud."

"Oh, Courtney dumped Liam all right. That part's true. But she's seeing some low-class grunge guy? Not so much."

Taryn quickly put in, "I kind of can't see Courtney going for someone who's not . . . uh . . . you know, rich. Like her."

Leesa scrunched her forehead. She might not be the brightest of the four, but she knew when Taryn was withholding. Or lying. Like now.

"If you want to know what I really think," Reign said, turning to look Leesa squarely in the eyes, "I think it's all a scam."

"What?" Leesa couldn't imagine where Reign was going with this.

"Courtney is blowing smoke in our faces and the K-Fed thing is the smokescreen," Reign said.

"You could be on to something there," Taryn said, unconvincingly.

"Still not following," Leesa said cautiously, eyeing Taryn.

Reign let out an impatient grunt. "She's covering the fact that she's hooked up with Brad! And furthermore, *she* probably planted the little item herself! We know how capable Courtney is of planting rumors. Bet anything *she* called Gossipmaven.com, which is where that numbskull Shelby got her big scoop from."

"But why would she plant a phony rumor about herself?" Leesa was beginning to wonder if this whole scene was a dream. Nothing connected.

"To throw everyone off the trail, of course!" Reign harrumphed. "How would it look if perfect, precious Princess Courtney went behind her best friend's back and stole her boyfriend? That's an image-wrecker for ya!"

Leesa's eyes widened as she gaped at Reign in dismayed disbelief. "Brad? And Courtney?" How could Reign think that? Courtney didn't even like Brad! "Get out!" she cried. "You're crazy!"

Reign plunked her elbows onto the table and buried her face in her hands. Which is when Leesa realized that Reign actually believed this bunk!

"Come on, Reign! You can't be serious!" Leesa insisted. "We're the Girls. We're like sisters. She wouldn't do that."

Leesa elbowed Taryn. "Courtney's not a backstabber. Come on, Taryn, tell her!"

Tiny Taryn did not, in fact, tell her. She just shrugged, and mumbled, "I guess it's possible . . ."

Reign looked at her with a sad, beaten expression.

Leesa had to do it. She didn't want to, but this whole thing had gotten way out of control. She hesitated. "Courtney's not seeing Brad, and I . . . I can prove it."

Taryn turned toward her so fast, Leesa thought she might get whiplash. "How? How . . . can you prove it?" she stammered.

Reign was intrigued. "You, Leesa Tenley, you can prove Courtney did not burgle my boyfriend. This oughta be a good one."

Burgle? What was she—oh, forget it. "Okay, I didn't want to tell you, because I didn't want to spoil the surprise. But, tough times call for . . . something."

"Just say it!" Reign exploded.

"Fine! I will! But remember, when your birthday comes around, you'll only have yourself, and your paranoia, to blame for spoiling the surprise."

Reign's expression didn't change. Nor did Taryn's.

"All right," she began, "the other day I saw Brad shopping in Blingtones for your birthday!"

Reign's eyes narrowed suspiciously. "What makes you think he was shopping for *me*?"

"Because he was with Star," Leesa revealed. "Would he take your sister with if he was buying something for another girl? I mean why would he need Star's opinion if he was getting something for Courtney?"

Reign had no comeback.

Nor did Taryn.

Finally, Reign said, "And you're sure of this? I mean, it's your store, so I guess you would be." She softened. "What'd he get?"

"You really do want your surprise ruined, don't you?"

Leesa told her. "It's a necklace, a star with a bonzo diamond in the center."

Like the sun coming out from behind a cloud, Reign's face lit up. "Cool."

And then Taryn, for some unfathomable reason, piped up. "And that's enough to make you believe he's not with Courtney? One little shopping trip? Maybe he just needed a girl's opinion, and Star was nearby. I think what Leesa just said doesn't add up the way you'd like it to."

Reign's face fell.

Leesa was aghast.

Taryn shrugged. "Sorry, I call it like I see it."

* * *

Leesa's head hurt. Mainly, from spinning. Taryn and Reign had split, leaving her with the bill and all the uneaten food. Leesa paid and asked the waiter to please wrap it up and send it to Loaves for Fish, the charity for the homeless, as it hadn't even been touched.

Air. She needed air, even if it was a desert hot Saturday in early November. Maybe a walk—albeit a short one; she was in Manolos, after all—would clear her head. How could Reign believe that Courtney and Brad were hanging out? How could Taryn totally lie, and agree with it? How could Shelby know anything at all?

The biggest question pounding at her was the simplest: how could Courtney break up with Liam? Why would she do that? He was the perfect package: sweet, sexy, scorching, sensitive. He sent flowers! He was attentive! He . . . he . . . made mix tapes for her! He didn't cheat, he was a gentleman, he didn't leer at her the way other guys did, either.

And Liam was smart, he had a future.

So what if he got drunk and went overboard once in a while? He was in college, it was totally normal! And besides, he'd apologized to Courtney for messing up her party—which seemed so long ago, now. Was she holding a grudge or something?

Making her way toward the front doors, Leesa walked through the casino slowly. And not, she thought huffily, because walking and thinking at the same time was a challenge. Her damn five-inch Manolos kept her pace slow. How she longed for the moment when stilettos would finally be out.

She passed the slot machines, where a woman with long honey-colored hair was feeding quarters and pressing the button simultaneously. It hit her—her brain was fried, and no one had thought of doing the most obvious thing: calling Courtney to get the truth!

She whipped out her cell phone. She was just about to hit 4, her speed-dial number for Courtney, when she spied someone familiar at the bar. His back was to her, but she'd know him anywhere. Buff, curly blond hair, Dockers on his feet, a drink in his hand, about to be poured down his throat.

She tapped him on the shoulder.

And one look told her it was true. Liam looked tragic. His pallor was gray, his eyes dull. If he weren't a guy, Leesa could have told him what kind of makeup—

"She left me." Liam started to cry, and Leesa wrapped her arms around him, as tightly as she could.

"Liam," she whispered, "come, let's get out of here. You're underage . . . and it's so public."

He shook his head. "Don't care. Let 'em arrest me. What've I got to lose? I already lost Courtney."

Leesa felt it was her duty to point out that he wouldn't be arrested, but the bartender, and the casino, could get in trouble. She knew Liam didn't care about that either, but she wanted to give him a shoulder to cry on. Somewhere private. She couldn't imagine Liam being humiliated if one of his frat buddies happened by. He was way too vulnerable right now.

Luckily, after one more shot of tequila, Liam allowed Leesa to lead him out of the Paris, and into her Porsche. She handed him a box of tissues and started the engine. She had no idea where to go, so she headed south on the interstate, toward the town of Primm. It was the only out-of-town waystation she could think of, the outlet mall that housed Last Call at Neiman Marcus.

On the drive, Liam began to open up. Followed immediately by beating himself up. "I should have seen this coming," he moaned.

"How could you have?" Leesa asked. "I mean, Courtney's so straight up, she's not deceitful. Usually."

Liam blew his nose and said wistfully, "She tried to tell me. She tried to break it off. But I just didn't think—I just didn't think she was serious. I talked her out of it, pretty much made it impossible for her."

Courtney had tried to break it off with him? That was news to Leesa. When they reached the outlet mall, Leesa wasn't sure what to do. She parked the car, and looked at Liam. "Want to, uh, go shopping?"

Well, at least that got a laugh out of him.

They ended up walking behind the mall, walking and talking, until Leesa finally said, "Can we sit somewhere? These shoes are killing me."

That was twice she'd made him laugh. Leesa was pretty sure that was a good thing. They found a concrete bench, where Liam leaned forward, his head in his hands.

He continued to talk. "It's just that she lied to me, man. She said she wanted to break it off because . . . well . . ." He paused, then decided to just go for it. "Because it'd be better for me if we were apart. That it wasn't fair to me to stay together."

Uh-oh. Leesa knew where this was heading, as any of the Girls would have. There was a song they liked to play, a country song by Terri Clark, called "Girls Lie, Too." And obviously, Courtney had demonstrated its veracity.

"She said because she wasn't ready to go all the way with me, that it wasn't fair to me. That I needed someone older, more willing. What a load of bull that turned out to be."

Leesa was truly taken aback. She hadn't known that Courtney and Liam didn't have sex. She'd always assumed that since they had something real going emotionally, the physical part was a gimme. Courtney had never told her Girls otherwise. And then, to tell Liam, "It's for your own good"? . . . that was as lame as "It's me, not you."

It hit Leesa hard, nearly as hard as it'd obviously hit Liam. Courtney was just not that into him.

"What happened, Liam?" she got up the nerve to ask.

"I came to see her. Her dad was out of town and asked me to check on her. I thought I'd surprise her, I brought . . . flowers! What a jerk I feel like."

He'd caught her. That was what'd happened. Courtney Bryant, smooth, cool, master of her domain, had been caught in the act—with someone else. Liam didn't say who, and Leesa was afraid to ask.

"So all the time she's telling me she's not ready to have sex with me, she's doing it with him!" Liam started to shake, to sob so hard just then, that Leesa could not find it in her heart to defend, or defile, her friend—nor to ask for any more details.

She simply held hunky, handsome Liam Mackenzie in her arms, until he was all cried out.

Chapter 18

A Father's Fury Unleashed!

The only time Taryn had left her bed was when she'd gotten the emergency text message from Leesa. It sounded like Court had been caught—and she had to make sure no one, not Leesa or Reign, suspected the truth. She'd promised Courtney she'd never tell anyone about Jake. But, dude, someone knew: Shelby Alexis, obviously. And she was about to spread it around town.

Taryn did what she had to.

She'd made Reign believe her ridiculous paranoia about Courtney and Brad was true. She'd made Leesa doubt herself. Worst of all, she'd called Shelby Alexis and debunked the rumor about the "low-class" kid Courtney was supposedly hooking up with. She told Shelby it was really Brad.

If she allowed herself time to dwell on what she'd done, the shitty feelings might override what was really depressing her:

the debacle with the Bones. But she reminded herself: Courtney and Jake had saved her sorry ass. The least she could do was keep their secret.

Even if it meant hurting another friend.

But could Reign be hurt when she'd find out soon enough that rumor wasn't true? And in the end, wasn't she really doing Reign a favor? Brad wasn't worth the stick of chewed-up gum she'd just tossed into the trash.

Life was too damn complicated.

After doing what she had to, Taryn climbed back into bed and resumed the one activity she'd been engrossed in for two weeks: staring at her ten-foot ceiling. She'd been in this position pretty much since the night of the Bones concert. When Courtney had brought her home, she'd walked straight to her bathroom, showered and washed her hair, pulled on a nightshirt, and climbed into bed. She'd lately thought of her home as a stifling, conformist trap. She suddenly realized that it was something else, too. It was safe—and Taryn felt an overwhelming need for that safety. At the risk of being booted out of school for absenteeism.

There was a knock at her bedroom door. "Taryn, you awake?"

Taryn sat up. She knew Courtney's voice. She'd called, of course, leaving a message for Courtney about what she'd done to stop the Jake rumor. So was Courtney here to thank her? Or rag on her?

Turned out it was neither. Courtney had laughed about the way Taryn had gotten Gossipmaven.com off the trail, and assured her, "I will straighten Reign out. As soon as she talks to me again. Not to worry."

Taryn wasn't sure what was different about Courtney as she watched her enter and perch at the edge of the bed. Had she actually gotten prettier? Was that even possible? Maybe that's what love does to you, she thought.

"So. You. Howzit hangin'?" Courtney asked, co-opting Taryn-talk. "Your mom came down on me about the low-life scum that we're allowing to perform at Delmonico's so I assume you told them what happened."

"I gave them the PG-13 version, anyway," Taryn confirmed. "He didn't succeed, thanks to you and Jake. I'd rather just forget it. He probably assumed I was a groupie and that's what I was there for."

"That," Courtney said sternly, "makes no difference. No girl is ever asking to be attacked. It wasn't your fault. The cops got him for drug dealing, so your parents don't have to know about the rest of it."

"Thanks," Taryn said. "I can't imagine how hurt my pops would be. You know, 'Conductor's Daughter Sexually Attacked by Drug Dealer!' "

Courtney caved kinda quickly, Taryn thought. Her gorgeous friend shrugged and said, "Do what you gotta do. Karma is Leesa's thing, but I have a feeling that monster's bad karma will come around to bite him in the end."

"I hope so," Taryn said thoughtfully.

"It might even all turn out for the best," Courtney said enigmatically.

"I don't see how it possibly could," Taryn grumbled. After so many weeks spent fixated on meeting the Bones, Fury in particular, the whole thing had been a complete disaster. She'd been lying in bed thinking about the fact that it was the second time she'd been attacked in less than two months. That surely had to indicate that she was on a wrong road. Her tough, flash and trash girl was no closer to her true self than the Little Miss Classical Musician Girl that her parents wanted her to be. Somewhere between those two opposite ends, the real Taryn Krakowski probably existed, though at the moment, she had no idea who that person actually was.

Enraged shouting suddenly erupted outside Taryn's bedroom. "Ivan! Stop!" Mynda Krakowski screamed. A piece of furniture crashed amid sounds of a major scuffle.

Taryn and Courtney flew out of the room. Hanging over the upstairs banister, Taryn saw her father, his silver hair wildly askew, attacking someone.

"Oh no!" Courtney gasped. "I left Fury standing in the front hall."

Taryn's mouth dropped in shock. "Fury?"

The girls stampeded down the stairs. "How dare you come here—you degenerate!" Ivan Krakowski bellowed.

"Dad!" Taryn shouted, throwing herself onto his raised arm. "He didn't have anything to do with it! He wasn't even in the room."

Fury was backed up against a wall, red-faced and breathing hard. His black leather jacket was half off. "That's true," he gasped, pulling the jacket back on. "I only just found out what happened. I flew here right after our Minneapolis gig to make things right, or just apologize. I'm sorry it took so long. I asked Courtney to bring me here so I could apologize on behalf of the group. We should have told you that night we were on the way out. But you were in your own world, you and your guitar. Man, if I realized you were with that dealer, I'd've clubbed the bastard myself."

Ivan Krakowski looked from his daughter to Courtney and back to Fury. "I can see no one is telling me the whole story, but clearly you are a person with morals." He offered his hand.

Fury shook it. "I try. I really want to apologize to Taryn, and to her family."

When her father had retreated to the living room, Taryn invited Fury to come in. "Can't," he declined. "I've got a jet to catch. We're playing Madison Square Garden tonight. I wanted you to know, though, that Eric is being indicted. One of the other girls who hangs with the band said he went after her, too."

"If she needs me to back her up, I will," Taryn offered.

"I'll tell her that."

Courtney began to back away from them. "I'm going to go ask Mr. Krakowski about tickets to his next concert. On behalf of my dad. He wants to go backstage so he can impress his new girlfriend. Be right back."

"I can't believe I just met Ivan Krakowski," Fury said, running his hand through his hair. Then he laughed ironically. "What a way to meet my childhood hero."

Taryn wasn't sure she'd heard him right. "No shit?"

"Don't get me wrong," he said with a laugh. "I idolized Sid Vicious and Johnny Rotten, the Ramones—dug Bono, too, still do . . . but Ivan Krakowski was the guy who first made me love music when I was a little dweeb studying classical guitar."

"I study classical guitar!" Taryn blurted. "I mean, before I quit."

"I could tell you knew your stuff," he complimented her.

"Yeah?" she asked, eagerly drinking in his words.

"Absolutely. You're the real deal. Sorry I had to run from the After Party—and again today for that matter. I'd love to hear your stuff. Do you have a demo?"

"No, but I'll make one," she assured him.

"Make sure you do," he said. "Courtney knows our manager's address. I'll tell him to look for it so it doesn't get lost." He took her hand in his. "Again, I'm really sorry about what happened. The guys pick up these druggie sleazeballs in every town we visit. It gives us a bad rep . . . but, hey, I guess that's life on the road."

"And I guess I'm not as ready for the road as I thought," she admitted.

"Nobody's prepared for what you went through. You've got the talent, though, and after a while you'll be able to see a bad situation coming and step aside before it hits you," he assured her kindly. "It comes with experience."

"Thanks," she said. He made it sound so possible. Maybe her dreams of rock stardom could come true, if she could manage to make it happen on her own terms.

"Take it cool and you'll get there," he added. "I've got to jet. Don't forget to send that demo." Cupping her chin, he kissed her lightly on the lips. "I'm looking forward to hearing it," he said.

Taryn believed him.

Chapter 19

So Busted

Reign had just gotten home from school. She'd stayed a little later than usual to prepare for an upcoming precalc test. She'd walked into her living room. And saw her sisters, Starshine and Haven.

And that's when everything went slo-mo on her.

Star stood at a window by the couch, her long, nearly black hair glistening in the sunlight. Her other sister, Haven, was across the room. Star scooped a pillow off the couch and playfully tossed it at Haven. Her eyes were bright with laughter and the pendant necklace around her throat swung out in front of her collarbone, seeming to hover for a second in midair. The diamond in the center of the necklace's golden star pendant caught the sunlight, gleaming brilliantly. Like a star. A *star* pendant for Star.

Leesa got half credit. Brad had gone shopping with Star—

but because he was shopping *for* Star! That was who he was hooking up with.

Her boyfriend was screwing *her* sister! It was suddenly so clear—and yet too heinous to possibly be true. Star was only fifteen—four years younger than Brad!

The slow-motion scene ended for Reign with the appearance of her mother, looking gorgeous as ever, albeit noticeably drawn and tense around the mouth, in a brocade Dior suit. "Girls, put those pillows back. I thought we were shoe shopping today."

"We're ready. We were waiting for you," Haven replied.

Lola turned to Reign. "Would you like to come?"

Too stunned by her revelation to speak, Reign shook her head and retreated to her room. Brad and Star? Brad and Star! BradandStarBradandStarBradandStar! It played over and over in her head until she thought she'd shatter into a billion fragments.

She would call him, but he never picked up anymore when he knew it was her. Of course, she usually called him from her cell phone, easily identifiable. Waiting until she heard the door close behind her mother and sisters, she called from the land-line in the now-empty living room.

"Hey, sweet cheeks," he answered.

She hesitated a moment. Sweet cheeks was his name for her. Did he know she was the one who was calling?

Had she been completely wrong? Hope ignited like a spark inside her. "Hello, Brad," she began.

Silence on the other end. "Star?" he asked uncertainly.

"Yes, it's me, Star," Reign went on, all hope dashed, replaced by a rage that caused her to dig her fingernails into her palms, completely oblivious to the pain. "I just had to call you."

"Missed me, huh?" he said smugly.

"Yes, and I'm worried about Reign. I think she's starting to suspect something."

"You didn't leave that box of Trojans out, did you?" he asked with a touch of panic.

"Trojans!" Reign screamed into the phone. He was making it with Star—all the way! "Brad, you are a disgusting pig! I hate you more than I've ever hated anyone in my whole life! You maggot! You're lower than scum! She's my sister, for God's sake." When she said the word "sister," her voice cracked and she began to cry. "She's my sister," she sobbed, "and she's only fifteen."

"I don't know why you're so bent out of shape. It's just a hookup!" he said, "It doesn't mean anything, right?"

"But why *her*?"

"You should consider it a compliment! Starshine is just like you—only with better hair, and more generous. But the truth is, she came on to me first."

Reign's knees turned to jelly. She managed, "I said it didn't matter what we did when one of us was out of town."

"That meant it didn't matter what *you* did," he corrected her, " 'cause I never *go* out of town so I have to get my out-of-town kicks *in* town. It was okay, you know. It's just sex and it's just a meaningless buzz."

Reign slammed down the phone and raced to her room, ready to sob her eyes out.

Only a funny thing happened on the way to pity-city. Like a fog lifting, a filmy veil peeled away, a focusing of the camera lens, for the first time in a long time, everything was very, very clear.

She'd been wrong. And so had Brad.

Brad's betrayal had nothing to do with her worthiness. And everything to do with the grubby, insensitive subhuman he was. He thought nothing of hooking up with Star, and the effect it'd have on her. He just didn't care. Why would she even want to be with someone like that?

Which led to another awakening. The casual hookup thing. Maybe some people could do it with random strangers, or have friends with benefits: But Reign del Castille was not "some people." She was deeper than that, more sensitive than that. She could, and had, been hurt by them.

Lesson learned.

That's when she cried.

What stopped the flow of tears, finally, was the noise of someone walking in the hall just outside her bedroom.

Cautiously, she got off the bed and peered through the opening of her partly closed door. Star! "What are you doing back here?" she demanded, stepping into the hall, her voice an angry growl.

Starshine turned back to her. "Mom and Haven were insisting on going to Lilly Pulitzer and I was so not interested, so I came back. I have to meet a friend in a little while, anyway."

"Who?" Reign barked. "Who do you have to meet?"

Starshine rolled her eyes. "None of your business."

Reign seethed inside as she advanced on her sister. She and Starshine had never been close—but they were sisters. Didn't that count for anything at all? Apparently it didn't, not to

Starshine. Brad's taunting words played over in her head: *Besides, she came on to me!*

"Nice necklace," Reign observed nastily, fingering the chain around her sister's neck. "Have a new boyfriend?" she spat as she flipped the pendant up so that it hit Starshine's chin.

Now Star knew. Her eyes flashed with momentary panic. Which passed quickly. She shrugged. "It's not like the two of you are together. Brad broke up with you—which made him fair game for me. I seized the moment."

No, little sister, the only thing you seized was the vermin—Brad's nothing but a parasite, wrapped in a pretty package, but ugly on the inside. He'll feed on you until he's had his fill, and then he'll walk away.

Reign said none of this. Star's toss of her shiny black hair, and superior attitude usurped any sisterly feelings she had just then. Her new clarity afforded her a glimpse of Star's real motive. Little sister was jealous of big sister, and wanted for herself what Reign had. How cliché!

But it reinforced Reign's newfound self-worthiness. All Star really had over her was the slender body and the hair. So dime-a-dozen in Vegas!

Starshine had none of Reign's spirit, her bold, daring attitude, her wicked sense of humor, her artistry, her uniqueness. Nor did Star have Reign's friends.

Little sister wanted Brad? Let her have him.

Star could leave . . . in a minute.

Reign seized a thick hank of Star's hair and used it to spin her around. With lightning speed, she yanked the necklace from Star's neck, sending it sliding along the hardwood floor.

Starshine gasped with horrified surprise and, before she could retrieve the necklace, Reign shoved her hard against the wall. The slap she intended to land on her sister's face missed its mark as Starshine rolled out of her grasp and disappeared into the bathroom. Reign swore, clutching her throbbing hand, which had hit the wall. "You can't hide from me," she yelled, going after Starshine.

She saw Starshine duck into the glass stall of the sauna/shower. "Dumb move. I've got you now!" she cried, pursuing her sister inside. Starshine was trapped and cowered in the corner of the stall.

"Girls! What's going on?"

Reign turned to see Lucinda, who had apparently been cleaning the whirlpool tub behind the shower. She stood in the doorway to the sauna with a bottle of spray bleach cleaner in her gloved hand and a stunned expression on her face. "What's all the shouting about?"

Without a word, Reign lunged for the spray bottle Lucinda held and grabbed it from her hand. She aimed it at Starshine's head, soaking her hair with the bleach.

Starshine whirled around to the wall, shoulders hunched, shielding her face with her hands. "Stop!" she shrieked. "It *burns*! Stop!"

Reign kept on, squirting and squirting as streaks of ugly, yellowish gray began streaking Starshine's once lustrous hair.

"Miss Reign! Please, stop!" Lucinda pleaded as she flailed her arms in a futile effort to wrest the squirt bottle from Reign's hand. It was useless. Reign was much taller and could easily keep the bottle away from her. "You can blind her! You must stop!"

The word "blind" cut into Reign's rage. How much did she want Starshine to pay for this? Enough to blind her?

Maybe. But no. Not really.

Besides, the ruined hair was gloriously hideous. It would do.

Starshine was crying with hysterical ferocity, her face still pressed against the tiles, as Reign handed Lucinda the bleach and left the bathroom. She trudged back to her bedroom and stretched out on her bed. And called Courtney.

When Shelby's Gossipmaven column had come out, telling the world that Courtney had betrayed her best friend by stealing Brad, Reign had felt enraged, humiliated, defeated. She'd never confronted Courtney directly, just stopped taking her calls, turned her back on her.

A wave of guilt engulfed her.

Courtney picked up the phone on the first ring. "What happened? You sound horrible," she intuited as soon as Reign spoke.

Tears choked Reign's voice as she told her about Brad and Starshine. "I'm so sorry I blamed you, but God, Court, it's like my whole family is falling apart."

Courtney's voice was hesitant. "You don't need to apologize. You've been going through some bummer times. But now that Brad's out of your life, maybe things will get better."

"You mean after the divorce?" There, she'd said it. Her parents had been really going at it lately. And Reign was sure her antics had something to do with it.

"I heard that rumor. If you believe the tabloids, or Gossipmaven, *everyone's* splitting up." Courtney was trying to sound hopeful.

"My mom blurted that Dad was cheating," Reign admitted tearfully. "And I think someone's asking him for money. I heard Mom say something like, 'Just give him the money and get rid of him!' Do you think someone's blackmailing him?" A horrible thought hit her. "Could it be Brad?" she wondered aloud. "Maybe he's threatening to sell a story about how he screwed the two daughters of Hollywood's power couple or something like that." The thought made her stomach twist into a knot.

"I don't know," Courtney replied. "Brad's a creep, but would he go as far as extorting money from your father? It's possible, I suppose."

"I wouldn't put it past him," Reign insisted. "You were right about him. He does have a gambling problem. He borrowed money from me."

"We'll make sure Brad pays for this," Courtney assured her.

"How?" Reign asked eagerly.

"Hmmm . . . Maybe Leesa, Taryn, and I could promise him a foursome in bed—you know, we show up in sexy underwear, get him all excited, cover him in honey, and tie him up."

"Are you kidding?!" Reign cried. "He'd love that!"

"And then we could dump a few ant farms on him and leave," Courtney concluded.

Reign guffawed with delighted laughter even though she'd been sure she'd never smile again. Her friendship with Courtney was an elixir.

"Perfect!" she crowed.

Chapter 20

The Girls Make a Splash!

Courtney swung her legs up onto the side of the russet couch in the Twi-Niter Lounge as she clicked off from her call with Reign. It'd left her more shaken than she wanted to admit.

The del Castilles had issues, but they didn't hold the patent on family dysfunction.

A boy had come between two sisters. A boy, if you could believe the scuttlebutt, had come between husband and wife. The same boy? Reign suspected so, but Courtney's intuition told her no. It wasn't Brad.

There are givers and takers in this world, Dan Bryant had taught her. Brad Simmons was a greedy, grabby, insensitive taker with a gambling addiction that one day would be his undoing, without any help from them. But he didn't have the balls—excuse the expression, she snickered to herself—to blackmail a movie star! He wasn't in that league, wouldn't know how to go about it. Stefan and Lola would laugh him right out of the house. And if that didn't work, their attorneys would scare the pants off the cretin.

Whoever was causing friction in Casa del Castille probably had something on Stefan and Lola from their past. No matter how outrageous and embarrassing Reign's behavior had been lately, Courtney didn't believe her friend had contributed to the family fissure.

Unlike, say, her own drama.

There were secrets at chez Bryant between Dan and herself. Some she was keeping, others were being kept from her.

Her father didn't know she was seeing Jake.

He refused to disclose why Jake was working at Delmonico's.

He'd never told her *why* her mom had left.

And Jake Martinez was keeping his real father's identity from her.

If you connected all the dots, those were the kind of secrets that could tear a family apart.

Courtney felt an acidic, sour taste creep up her esophagus, into her throat. It was accompanied by an acidic, poisonous thought. She fought to quell them both. Because it just wasn't possible.

She leapt off the couch and flipped open her laptop. Googling "Jake Martinez" probably wouldn't get her anywhere. But she did it anyway. She suddenly had a burning need to know the identity of this rich, powerful benefactor. Was the man paying for his tuition at Brighurst really his father? If so, why didn't he just come forward and take Jake in? And if he wasn't, what *was* the relationship? And what did it have to do with the waiter gig at Delmonico's?

Unsurprisingly, Google turned up nothing. She tried "Rosa Martinez." Here she got a tiny nibble. She learned that the woman had died, just when Jake said, the previous August. She uncovered the interesting tidbit that Rosa had worked, for a stretch of time, in Las Vegas. As a housekeeper. It did not say who her employer had been.

Courtney knew how to access the hotel's employee records. They went back pretty far. If Rosa had ever worked there, it'd be listed. There might be a notation in Jake's file, too—about who asked for him to get the job.

Courtney swallowed hard. If Jake didn't want her to know, should she go all Sydney Bristow and find out anyway? The records had always been right there, at her fingertips. If she'd wanted to access them at any time, she could have.

Her finger on the mouse, she pointed the curser to the Human Resources icon on her laptop and held her breath. Answers might be a double-click away. Until tonight, Courtney had been able to bury any suspicions she might've had in her subconscious.

Right now? After getting off the phone with Reign? Not so much.

Cohesive sentences popped into her brain, and once there, they couldn't be submerged again. What if her father hadn't hired Jake as a favor to anyone at all? What if Dan Bryant himself was Jake's father?

The idea was so sickening, she clutched her stomach and ran for the bathroom. It would explain why her father had lied to her. It would explain why Jake was here, at the Del. It would explain why Dan forbade her to see him.

But it would mean, oh God, no, she was sleeping with her

own brother. A treacherous boy who knew exactly what he was doing: her undoing.

"Courtney, are you all right?" Dan Bryant, dapper in a casual blue Paul Smith shirt and black pants, was standing in the doorway of her bathroom, looking concerned. "Sweetheart, are you sick?"

Courtney wiped her face with a soft towel doused in warm water, and stared at him. "That depends," she said evenly, "on the answer to the question I'm about to ask you."

Dan furrowed his brow. He put his hands on her shoulders and drew her to him. "Courtney, what's the matter? What's going on?"

She shook off his embrace, folded her arms defensively. "I need you to be brutally honest with me."

"Can I be honest in the living room? I'm not big on bathroom confessions."

"Not funny, Dad," Courtney muttered, but allowed him to guide her back inside. Dan settled on the sofa, and crossed his legs. She refused to sit next to him. Or sit at all.

"Is Jake Martinez your son?"

"Whaaat?" Dan coughed. "That's what you think? Courtney, if I had another child, why would I hide it from you?"

"You lied to me. First you said Bill Martin hired him, but I know for a fact that you did. Then you say, oh yeah, you did hire him—as a favor to a friend. But you won't say who, or why. Then you forbade me to see him—"

Alarmed, her father interrupted, "You're seeing him?"

"Dad!" Courtney was shouting now. "Are you his father? Yes or no?"

"No!" Dan exploded, springing off the couch.

"I don't believe you," she said, wavering now.

"That's outrageous!"

"It's *not* outrageous!" she kept on. "Clearly, you're hiding something."

Her dad began to pace, an indication he was trying to think of what to say.

"Why did my mother leave?" Courtney asked accusingly.

Dan stopped in his tracks and narrowed his eyes, the same hue of aqua as Courtney's own. "You think I had an affair, an affair that produced an illegitimate child. This Jake . . . who suddenly turns up here?"

Courtney stuck out her chin. "Tell me it's not true."

Dan took her hand firmly, and sat her back down on the couch. Softly, he said, "Sweetheart, your mom left me because she fell head over heels for some other guy. She went with him to the Midwest somewhere."

"*She* was cheating?" Courtney asked doubtfully.

"Yes. Women cheat, too, you know. No matter who's doing it, there's a world of hurt involved, worse when there are kids."

She would have asked him why he never told her. But Courtney was not about rhetorical questions. He hadn't told her because he'd never wanted to hurt her. So Jake had been right—her mother *had* abandoned her. This guy she took off with was more important than her two-year-old daughter.

She leaned into her father's chest. He smelled of the new cologne she'd gotten him, Aqva by Bvlgari.

"Can you tell me who you did the favor for?" she asked, still burying her head in his chest. "Who Jake's father is?"

Dan took a deep breath. "I made a promise to a friend. A

vow. And I know that you, better than anyone, can understand why I won't break it. Friends, and family—it's all we have, Courtney. The most precious gifts of our lives."

* * *

Courtney and her father had an early dinner à deux that night, out on their private terrace. It was the first time in weeks they'd dined together, and in honor of the occasion, they turned their phones off. No interruptions. Over a simple spread sent up by the kitchen staff of salad, steaks, fries, and red wine, Courtney caught him up on the Brighurst happenings, and Dan caught her up on his latest girlfriend. It was too early to tell, he assured his daughter, whether this was a serious relationship or not. When he asked the Jake question, Courtney volleyed, "Right back atcha, Dad. It's too new to know."

Dan sipped his wine. "Okay, Courtney, I'll butt out. But I want you to know that the reason I'm not in favor of you and Jake has nothing to do with the fact that he works here, or that his heritage is different from ours."

She quipped, "Yeah, you don't care that he's got no money, and is about as far from a prep as Liam is from a grunge rocker!"

Dan appreciated the comparison. "From what I hear, the kid's got some good qualities. He takes his work seriously, seems to have fit in with the staff, and so far, I haven't heard of any problems at school."

Courtney joked, "Well, that's a ringing endorsement if I ever heard one!"

"What do you want from me, Courtney? I don't really know him."

"Then what's the objection to me seeing him?"

"Sweetheart, you just have to take me at my word. It's complicated. That's all I can say."

Later, after her dad went down to the casino, she turned her phone back on. There were several missed calls, from Reign, Taryn, and Leesa. She rang Reign first, who picked up right away. Courtney heard gurgling sounds in the background, laughter, and . . . water splashing?

"Where are you?" Courtney wondered what pool they were at.

"Where are *you?*" Reign parried back. "Been trying to call—didn't you get my messages? Wait—someone wants to sing to you."

"*I'm always chasing waaa-ter-faalls.*" It was Taryn, warbling some cheesy tune, giggling hysterically.

Okay, her Girls had obviously had a few drinks. But where were they?

Reign returned to the phone. "We're getting baptized," she roared gleefully, "celebrating new beginnings. Life without Brad, mainly!"

"Okaaay . . ." Courtney said warily. "Are you in a wave pool somewhere?"

"Better than that!" Reign revealed. "We're in the middle of the waterfalls! Whoosh! Taryn," she shouted gleefully, "stop splashing! You'll drown my cell phone!"

Oh. My. God. They were dancing in the brand-new waterfalls of the Wynn Las Vegas Resort and Country Club, one of the glitziest on the Strip. Courtney'd seen the spectacle, forty-five feet high, set into an eight-story mountain covered with thousands of pine trees. Tiers of rushing waterfalls gushed into a three-acre lagoon—it was the signature sight at the hotel. It was meant to be gazed at with awe, like the dancing fountains at the Bellagio. It was so *not* meant for people to prance through, dance in, swim in, or use for symbolic baptism!

Taryn was back to her old subversive self, and Reign was ready to be tabloid-bait again. Oh yes, things were definitely getting back to normal!

"Come on!" Reign was saying. "Get your butt down here! Leesa's on the way, this is big-ass fun!"

Steve Wynn would have a conniption when he found out. Dan Bryant would get a call. *She'd* better get her tush in gear! She, too, had something to celebrate: Jake was free and clear—relatively speaking!—to be her boyfriend, and best of all, she no longer had to hide their relationship from her father.

Energized by the idea of being with her Girls, and checking out the Wynn competition at the same time, Courtney was all over it. "Meet you in half an hour!" she chortled before getting off the phone.

Out of habit, she grabbed the remote and turned the TV on as she walked toward her ginormous closet. What does one wear to prance through waterfalls, and then possibly, be hauled off to the city jail?

Hmmm . . . this did call for some serious thinking. She got Leesa on the phone, who was already on her way over to the Wynn. Her favorite fashionista hinted that she, too, had something to celebrate tonight. She wanted to share her good news with everyone . . . and no, she wasn't going to tip off Courtney first.

On Leesa's advice, Courtney chose a new color-swirl Pucci

bikini, white capris, and pink Cole Haan slides. She was deciding on which cover-up to wear over the bikini top when she chanced to look up at the TV. The big-screen plasma was tuned to *E! True Hollywood Story.* The subject was Oscar-winning actor Stefan del Castille. She chuckled as she went into the bathroom to put her hair up in a Pebbles Flintstone scrunchie and get with the waterproof mascara.

When she returned, the face on the big-screen TV stopped her in her tracks—her hand flew across her open mouth. The E! documentary was detailing Stefan's arrival in the United States, and the photo of him, at eighteen, was taken from his very first film.

The face on-screen was a dead ringer for Jake Martinez.

* * *

Courtney sprang into action. She threw a Juicy sweatshirt over her bikini top and dashed to the elevator. Jake was working tonight at Nishimira, the Del's most upscale restaurant. Safe to say the entire place did a double take as Courtney blasted in, babbling to Bill Martin that she was sorry, he'd have to find someone to cover tonight for Jake: she needed him now. It was a full-on emergency. If her dad's longtime staff boss was annoyed, he didn't show it.

Jake, however, did. "What are you doing? This is embarrassing!" he protested as she led him out of the restaurant, then through the casino and the lobby. Outside, she whistled for the Del limo.

"We have somewhere to be," she told him earnestly. "I'm sorry I stealthed you, but there are some secrets that have been kept for too long. Unlike wine, they don't get better with age.

They get rotten, and infectious." The limo pulled around, and Courtney opened the door. "Get in, Jake. Please."

Jake slid across the leather seats warily, as he pondered her words. As soon as the driver closed the door behind him, he turned to her. Snap! His face registered comprehension.

He knew. Without her having to explain, Jake Martinez knew precisely what Courtney was doing. And why.

"How'd you find out? Did your dad tell you?"

"No, Jake, he didn't betray Stefan's secret. But tabloid TV?—can't trust 'em. We should be relieved they're too superficial to explore further."

At his puzzled expression, she said, "E! The True Hollywood Story of Stefan del Castille.' A retrospective of his career, starting when he was just about your age."

Jake pursed his lips. "And now we're going to tell Reign?"

"We're going to tell everyone. About everything."

"Courtney"—he squeezed her hand—"don't take this the wrong way, but are you sure it's your business to tell her? This is huge."

Courtney's heart did an involuntary flip-flop. She was *so* into him. "As long as it's okay with you, we tell her. So, Jacob Martinez, are you down with this?"

He took his time answering. "The more I get to know Reign, well, chica, she *needs* a big brother. But . . ."

"What? We're almost there, Jake. Speak now, or I'm gonna do this thing. Did Stefan forbid you to say anything?"

"No, no, he's not like that. If it were up to him, I'd probably be living in the mansion now, embraced by the family. Only—"

"—Lola refused?" Courtney guessed.

"I refused."

Courtney ventured, "Because your mother didn't want his money, you don't want it either? Is that why? The pride thing?"

"That, yeah. But also I don't want to be the one responsible for the train wreck, man. It'll be blown all over the tabloids, and the family could break up—she could divorce him, the kids could hate him. I don't want that on my head."

Courtney cupped his face in her hands. God, she loved him.

"I'm hereby taking it on *my* head. Reign needs to know what's going on; she's confused, freaked out about her family. Stefan and Lola are actors. Movie stars. I'm not judging them, but sometimes their self-absorption level is off the chart and doesn't leave them room to consider others—even if the others are their own children."

"While you, on the other hand, always have Reign's best interests at heart? No matter what the consequences?" he challenged.

"I'm her best friend, Jake. That means everything."

* * *

Amazingly, her Girls had not been caught by Wynn security and tossed into the clinker. Reign and Taryn, wearing only their skivvies, had been joined by a bikini-clad Leesa. They were playing tag, dashing through the pools, under and around the waterfalls, singing, laughing, splashing around. Like carefree kids. Courtney could not believe they hadn't been tossed out on their shapely asses. What up with security?

As the limo dispatched them in front of the sleek coppery Wynn tower, Courtney grabbed Jake's hand and dashed over to her Girls.

Taryn lit up. "Duuuude! You brought him!" She was sloshed, in more ways than one.

Leesa glowed, and jumped up and down, obviously busting to tell her secret.

Reign tilted her head, eyeing Jake in his waiter uniform. "We'll have four hypnotiques, with Früs vodka. I'm over Ketel One and Red Bull—so yesterday!" She splashed both of them.

Courtney laughed and grabbed Jake's arm. "On three?"

Jake grinned. "One . . . two . . ."

Courtney kicked off her slides, Jake his loafers, and they jumped in together. Taryn immediately dashed up behind them and, with Reign and Leesa's help, pushed them under the tallest waterfall.

Completely soaked, Courtney finally said to Reign, "We have something to tell you."

"Workin' it with the waitstaff, huh?" Reign chortled. "Can he get us our drinks first?"

Courtney put her arms around Jake, tilted her head up, and gave him the kind of kiss that could not be misinterpreted.

Reign's eyes went huge. "You guys? You're . . . together?"

Leesa kicked water in Reign's face. "See, I told you there was no smokescreen. That Courtney wasn't pretending to be with someone else because she was really seeing Br—"

"Do! Not! Say his name," Reign cautioned, "unless you want a face plant in the lagoon."

Courtney narrowed her eyes. "Taryn was the only one who knew. And she purposely told Shelby a lie, so Gossipmaven.com would be discredited. How did you find out?"

Leesa put her hands on her hips and stuck her chest out proudly. "My boyfriend told me."

It was Courtney's turn to go slack jawed. For a second, that is, until she understood fully. Then a megawatt smile emerged, brighter than the spotlights on the waterfall. "You and Liam. Oh, my God! You guys are perfect together! Why didn't I ever see that?"

"Maybe because you were seeing him?" Taryn teased.

Courtney tossed a handful of water in Taryn's face, then dashed over to give Leesa a hug. "You were always there for him, Leese. He's a great guy."

"And don't take this the wrong way, Courtney," Taryn put in, "but he's over you."

Courtney started to chase Taryn, but the small girl was too fast for her. Jake, whose shirt clung to his abs, came up and put his arms around her waist, nuzzling her cheek.

It was time.

Courtney clapped her hands and called her Girls over. "We have something else to tell you. Well, to tell Reign mostly."

Reign ran her fingers through her messy sopping hair. "I'm feeling too good for anything you say to bum me out—so bring it."

Courtney took a deep breath. "You know how you're always saying you wished you had a brother?"

* * *

Security finally tossed the quintet out. Only Courtney's cachet kept them from having their parents called or, worse, being hauled off in a squad car. She even sweet-talked them into bringing out towels for her group, promising not to inform anyone exactly how long it'd taken security to discover their antics.

Soaked, stunned, brimming with a million questions,

Reign, Taryn, Leesa, Courtney, and Jake simply plopped themselves down on the sidewalk, right in the middle of Las Vegas Boulevard.

And explained everything.

It took Reign a long time to get through to her father, en route to a location shoot in Africa. She finally got him on the plane. Stefan confirmed everything, begged forgiveness—and promised a huge family powwow as soon as he got back. "The whole family," he said.

"And Mom's okay with this?" Courtney heard Reign ask dubiously.

"We're a family, we'll pull together."

Reign reported her father's parting words after she hung up. Jake put his arm around her, and grazed her forehead. "Hey, sis . . . if you ever want to talk, any time. But I think I'm gonna split now. Kinda feels like the four of you—'Girls'—maybe could use some alone time."

Courtney jumped up. He was so sensitive! "I'll get the limo to take you back"—but Jake held his palms up. "No. Once was enough for me. I'll walk."

* * *

Courtney did ask the limo driver to come over; she sent him for a bottle of Cristal and four champagne flutes. As the traffic crawled by in front of them, gawking tourists, high rollers, and women of the night stepped around them. The Girls sipped their bubbly, alternately bubbling with enthusiasm and full of chagrin, stomach-twisting anxiety, and doe-eyed dopey love.

"You know what Liam says about me?" Leesa shared.

"That you put out?" Taryn taunted. Earning her a kick in the shins from both Leesa and Courtney.

"Liam thinks my body is perfect just the way it is. He says all I have to do to be beautiful is breathe. Isn't that . . . like, the most amazing thing anyone's ever said?"

Courtney gave Leesa a hug. "That is amazing. And true, Leesa. I wish it hadn't taken a guy for you to see it, is all. A mirror would've done just fine."

"Is there somewhere for me to puke?" Taryn said, lifting her champagne glass to her lips. "I can only do so much mushy before I hurl."

Courtney grinned. "Good to know you're back to full emotional health."

"Well, not all the way back," Taryn advised.

"Meaning?" Leesa asked.

"I talked to my pops. He's willing to deal. I think the visit from Fury impressed him. That, and listening to the demo tape I made. Don't get me wrong, he's still got Juilliard on the brain, but there might be some wiggle room in there. We'll see what the next few months brings."

"At least you're talking," Leesa burbled. "That's so fabulous!"

Reign sighed. "This is what we have to put up with now? Leesa in hyperbole land?"

Courtney took Reign's hand. "It's you we've all been most worried about. Are you—do you think you're gonna be okay? It *is* really a great thing that you cut Brad loose. But . . ."

Reign folded her arms. "Okay, we're not gonna do the respect-yourself speech, okay? I have a lot to deal with first. My backstabbing little sister, for one—"

"You know he'll hurt her, too," Courtney pointed out.

Reign chuckled. "Yeah, especially now that her hair's kinda messed up. Streaked, you might say."

They'd downed two bottles of Cristal before Reign poured her heart out. She didn't want her family to break up because of Jake. Deep in her heart, she didn't want Star to get hurt by someone as unworthy as Brad. And she was starting to think that she might put her random hookups on pause for a while. "They're meaningless," she insisted, "but that doesn't mean you can't get hurt by them."

Courtney, Taryn, and Leesa didn't tease, taunt, or interrupt. They did, however, pinky swear they'd never tell. If Reign was going wholesome—no one else would ever know!

They were the Girls. Secrets would stay with them.